Monster Town

Bruce Golden

This edition contains the complete text of the original hardcover edition.

PUBLISHING HISTORY
PS Publishing Ltd. hardcover edition / August 2017
PS Publishing Ltd. e-book edition / October 2017
Shaman Press paperback edition / October 2019
Shaman Press e-book edition / October 2019

ISBN-13: 9781697181975

Shaman Press

http://goldentales.tripod.com/

Also by Bruce Golden
MORTALS ALL
BETTER THAN CHOCOLATE
EVERGREEN
DANCING WITH THE VELVET LIZARD
RED SKY, BLUE MOON
TALES OF MY ANCESTORS
AFTER THE END [upcoming}

The humorous story is told gravely; the teller does his best to conceal the fact that he even dimly suspects that there is anything funny about it.

Mark Twain

It's alive! It's alive!

Dr. Henry Frankenstein

Monster Town

Toto, I've a feeling we're not in Kansas anymore.

Dorothy

1

THE BLOOD OF HIS BLOOD

I t was a hard wet rain that beat an ominously staccato rhythm on the roof of my Packard as I drove to the outskirts of the city. Thunder rumbled overhead like a bowling ball sliding down a corrugated tin roof, and I imagined the ferocious whipcracks of lightning tearing great rents in time and space.

The rain didn't bother me. Neither did the thunder. I was sober . . . more or less. What nagged me was the unknown. Not the unknown I knew about. I could deal with that. It was the obscure unknown — the one that always popped its ugly mug out of a dark shadow with a cackling laugh — that worried me. Call it a personality quirk, but I could never be completely relaxed if there was a mystery to be solved — even if I knew the answer would presently reveal itself.

What puzzled me this particular evening was what the wealthiest man in town wanted with me. Usually I just took pictures of cheating spouses or an occasional insurance scammer pretending to be laid-up, but actually water-skiing off Catalina. However, three hours ago I'd gotten a call from some secretary saying her boss, one Vladimir Prince, would like to speak with me about contracting my services. What the job was, she wouldn't say, asking only that I arrive precisely at seven. I almost said no thanks, as I'd planned on being deep inside a bottle by seven. Normally I never let my work interfere with my drinking, but the rent was due.

You may or may not know that Vladimir Prince was the owner of several wineries and a couple breweries, along with enough other businesses and real estate holdings to choke a platoon of accountants. Unless you keep up with the trades, you probably *don't* know that Prince feathered his initial nest egg working in the movie business. He was known back then as "Dracula" or "Count Dracula" or "the Dark

Prince," depending on the script. Unlike most horror movie stars, he'd invested wisely. Which is why he lived out on the very edge of Monster Town, away from the urban blight and general riffraff that infested its main streets.

Of course Monster Town isn't the way most people picture it. Yes, it had its roots in a time when movie monsters were ostracized by their Hollywood brethren. Instead of fighting to fit in, they let themselves be ghettoized just south of Beverly Hills, into a postwar industrialized area whose industries had gone belly up. And it wasn't just famous freaks of the silver screen who lived there. It was also home to hundreds—hell, *thousands* of wannabes. It wasn't unlike Hollywood in that sense—where every waitress is a star-in-waiting, and every valet has a screenplay he wants you to read.

Yes, Monster Town, for the most part, is populated with the hopeful, the star-struck, the dregs of the Earth who weren't quite monstrous enough. Its avenues are peppered with the gimps, the geeks, the oddballs, and the mutants who never got their shot at fame and fortune. Some of the better-known monsters reside there too, though few of them were as smart or successful as Prince. What they have are their memories, their dog-eared posters, their faded fame . . . but little fortune.

Casting directors still, on occasion, trolled the streets for a small part here and there, but Tinseltown just wasn't making monster flicks like they used to. So, when the celluloid gravy train dried up, monsters had to make a living like anyone. Now they were fry cooks and teachers and dogcatchers and shopkeepers. Some were hoodlums, others thieves, and a few were even killers. In other words, Monster Town was really like any other city.

Before I could get to the suburb I was headed for, I had to pass through the ghost town that had been the old factory district. Most of the companies there had gone out of business years ago, but I saw a few still showing signs of life. Whether they were actually making things or just tearing them down, I had no idea. I passed the old pump station and was surprised to see it still pumping away, despite its rusted exterior, diverting water from the L.A. County Waterworks' main line to Monster Town. I guess something had to keep the toilets flushing.

Even though I lived in Monster Town, I wasn't in show business — never had been. I ended up there by happenstance. Not really an interesting story. Now I was just looking for a job to pay my bills and keep me in hooch. Though I never imagined a job would take me this far from the grime and crime of the city's venal core.

Even when I was flush with cash I didn't get out of town much. I certainly was never invited to any parties in the ritzy neighborhood I was driving through at that moment. I belonged there like broccoli belongs on a chocolate sundae. But the trees and green grass were a nice change from the littered asphalt and peeling paint I could see from my own digs. The fresh air wouldn't hurt me either, though I figured I shouldn't make a habit of it.

The truth is, it was almost a dreamscape. Each house I drove past seemed bigger and more ostentatious than the last. When I finally reached Prince's place, it was, without a doubt, the biggest one yet. You couldn't even call it a house. It was a full-blown mansion — a pearly-white summer palace standing iridescent in the rain.

I gave my name at the gate and was granted entry. The rain slowed to a damp drizzle, and the sky cleared just enough to reveal the setting sun. I didn't know if it was the still-lingering clouds or the fact I needed another drink, but it felt like an uncertain gloom had settled over the lush countryside. The only thing I was confident of, was that I needed new windshield wiper blades.

I pulled into the estate and took a look around.

Its grounds were manicured as carefully as a duchess in waiting. Guards patrolled the extended property with sentry dogs. I shuddered just a little. I didn't like dogs — not guard dogs, not poodles, not friendly little mutts. I wasn't afraid of them. I just didn't like them. Fortunately there were none close to the house where I was told to park. I pulled up and got out of the Packard. I put on my hat and adjusted my trench coat.

Maybe it was just the extravagance of the setting, or the idea I'd be sitting down with the richest man in town, but I noticed the old fedora was getting a bit threadbare. That made me think about my coat, and the stain on it from that night I couldn't remember. Well, he wasn't hiring me for fashion advice . . . if he was even hiring me at all.

Because of the way it was built, you had to look up to really see Prince's stately manor in its entirety. Framed there by somber, billowing clouds, it was like a purposely awe-inspiring establishing shot some B-movie director had composed. I didn't know if it was more menacing than it was pretentious, but it reeked of intrigue and danger, with its massive columns and interlacing arches rising up like some old southern slave plantation. I stared up at it and could almost hear a mysterious, forlorn sax wailing in the background, backed by a handful of enigmatic violins—a film score in my head.

Out front there was actually an open tent designed just for a car. Underneath it was a Rolls Royce. A manservant was busy polishing the driver's side. I noticed the usual female "Spirit of Ecstasy" hood ornament had been replaced with a sterling bat, its wings outstretched in an imitation of flight. It was weird, but definitely appropriate.

Before I reached the stairs leading up to the manor's entrance, four guys in expensive suits came walking out of the huge double doors. They weren't monsters, at least on the outside, and I'd never seen them before. I waited until they got into a limo that was waiting for them and drove off.

I trudged up the stairs, breathing harder with each step and thinking a little exercise now and then wouldn't kill me. It didn't help that the rain always made my old wound ache.

Catching my breath, I rang the bell. Faintly I heard something from inside that sounded like the summoning of the monks. It was only seconds before the doors opened. Standing there was this guy dressed like a cross between an opera singer and a 17th Century French general. I recognized him right away from his movie days, when he played Renfield, Dracula's servant in all those old films. Apparently some actors couldn't shake their erstwhile roles.

He stood there for a moment, staring at me with blatant disdain, before saying, "Mr. Slade, I presume."

"That's right. I'm here to see Mr. Prince."

His bug eyes reminded me of Peter Lorre. Using them to full advantage, he gave me another look like he might have to disinfect the place if he let me in. Resigned to it, he stepped aside so I could enter. I caught a whiff of gun oil as I passed him. He had it hidden well, under that costume of his, but I figured he was packing.

"May I take your hat and coat?" he asked in a manner that told me he didn't really want to touch them.

"No, thanks," I said. "I'll keep them."

It was a grand entryway, wide open and almost high enough for King Kong to stand without slouching. A huge staircase dominated the space, its lacquered railings leading up and around to where they finally vanished from view. The decor was all ivory and chrome—not at all what I expected from the Prince of Darkness.

Renfield directed me to the library, which, with its hundreds of books, looked like any other millionaire's library—I presumed, having never really been in one. I wondered how many of the books Prince had actually read. My first thought was, probably not many—though if the rumors about his age were true, he just might have had the time to read them all.

"Wait here," instructed Renfield. "The master will be with you shortly."

I looked the place over. It was cluttered with woodcarvings, little stone statues, and other eccentric doodads. There was a large fireplace with an ebony gargoyle perched on cither end of the mantel, a finely crafted antique work desk, and some overstuffed chairs. But what dominated the room was above the mantel. It was a life-sized portrait of Prince himself. From what I remembered, it was a perfect likeness.

It featured his aristocratic nose, his close-set black eyes, and that famous stare of his that would have frozen a hot cup of joe.

Nosey sleuth that I was, I wandered over to the desk and looked at the papers scattered there. I was surprised to see a brochure from that new amusement park they'd recently built down in Anaheim—the one I figured was mostly for kids. It didn't seem like a place Dracula would visit for fun. Yet there was a map of the place and some design schematics I couldn't quite make out.

I didn't want to touch anything, so I twisted my head around to get a better look. I was only half twisted when a voice surprised me.

"I thought I'd come down and get a look at you myself."

Standing in the doorway was a sleek dame decked out in a simple white satin dress that likely cost more than my Packard did new. She was a looker, and by the way she stood posed there, she knew it. She had dark hair, sophisticated eyes, and pouty lips, but her face was pale . . . almost sickly looking.

Out of reflex, I took off my hat. I don't think she cared.

"So you're the private detective." It wasn't a question, so I didn't answer. "I thought gumshoes only existed in movies."

"I'm real enough . . . but it usually takes me a couple of belts to get warmed up."

She flashed a quick smile and sauntered towards me with sufficient sex appeal to stir a eunuch. When she was close enough for me to smell her perfume, she stopped. She reached out to touch my chest with her finger, as if to be certain I wasn't an illusion.

I wasn't sure what she'd try to touch next, but I thought it best to remain professional and not find out. I took hold of the hand she'd stroked me with and gave it a little shake.

"Dirk Slade. Pleased to meet you. Are you Mr. Prince's daughter?"

She giggled at some private amusement as I released her hand.

"Mr. Prince doesn't have any daughters . . . that I know of," she said, staring up at me with a wantonness that was hard to miss.

"I see you've greeted our guest, Mina."

I looked up from her beckoning eyes and saw him. I'd expected him, I knew I'd be meeting with him, but to actually see him in the flesh was a shade unsettling. I mean, how often do you find yourself in the presence of Count Dracula? Even if he was just an old actor, he was still the grand monarch of monsters.

"Now please," he said to her with only a slight accent, "I need to speak with Mr. Slade alone."

She pouted but it was a little girl act that faded quickly to an alluring smile. She waved her fingers at me and walked out.

He waited until she was gone and said, "My son doesn't approve of my paramour. He thinks she's too young."

It's true she didn't look half his age—and that's if he was only as old as he looked.

"However, like many people, I'm a creature of my desires. And I've always had an indescribable thing for girls named Mina. She's not particularly bright, but she pleases me in the ways that matter most."

I briefly speculated on what those ways were, but realized I probably didn't have the imagination to do it justice.

He moved towards me then. I say *moved* because he seemed to glide more than walk. He was as smooth as milk on marble and right next to me with his hand out before he should have been.

"Vladimir Prince," he said, taking hold of my hand but not shaking it. "Pleased to make your acquaintance." He'd let go of my hand and was making his way around his desk before I knew it. "You come highly recommended, Mr. Slade." His voice was gently commanding, yet reassuring.

"Please, have a seat." He gestured at the chairs in front of his desk.

"Who recommended me?" I was curious who would vouch for me with a high roller like Prince.

"Oh I know many people, Mr. Slade. I have many sources."

"I'm a fan of yours, as well," I said. "I've seen all your—"

"Please," he said a bit too loudly. "Let's let the past stay in the past. I'd rather speak about the matter at hand."

Apparently he didn't want to talk about his old movies. Maybe the association was bad for business. That was jake with me, so I took a seat.

"What *is* the matter at hand? I was told you were in need of my services."

He hesitated and I took the moment to study him more carefully.

He was slender, with short, slicked-back dark hair and a pasty complexion, not unlike his young squeeze. He wasn't wearing the cape I half expected, but looked refined in a very expensive, stylishly embroidered smoking jacket. The only thing out of place about him were his long fingernails. Whether he sharpened them to a point or they just grew that way, I had no idea.

He still hadn't answered me, so I reached into my coat pocket. Before I even touched my pack he said, "Please don't smoke."

Renfield appeared then, carrying a tray filled with an elaborate bone china tea set and some little biscuits.

"Would you join me in tea?"

The tea really threw me. I found his choice of beverage surprising for a guy whose empire was built on booze. If anything, I expected him to offer me a mug of Impale Ale, or maybe a glass of Vlad's Sangria.

To be polite, and because I really needed this job—whatever it was—I picked up one of the dainty cups of tea Renfield had poured and took a sip. I was almost afraid my big mitt would crush the little thing.

"Before I tell you why I've asked you here today, Mr. Slade, I must be certain I can count on your discretion."

"I'm as discreet as they come, Mr. Prince. I wouldn't last long in this business if I wasn't."

He sipped his own tea and I watched the shadowed corners of his mouth, hoping for a glimpse of those famous canines of his. I didn't see them. I did notice his face held this cool, controlled expression that never seemed to change. Not even when he began to tell me why I was there.

"My son has gone missing, Mr. Slade. I want you to find him."

"How old is he?"

"John is 17."

"How long's he been missing?"

"Three weeks now."

"If you don't mind my saying, it seems like a long time to wait before trying to find him."

He got this faraway look in his eyes. "My son has been known to make himself unavailable for days at a time. You might say I was unconcerned I hadn't heard from him, at least until recently."

"Why not call the police?"

"I don't want the police involved. I'm sure you understand."

I nodded. There could be a dozen reasons why he didn't want the police in on this. Half of them legitimate.

"Alright, I'll take the job. I get a hundred dollars a day," I said, doubling my normal fee, "plus expenses."

He waved his hand as if cost was an insignificant detail.

"Any idea where I should start looking for your son?"

"I know he has a school friend at James Whale High named Harold Talbot. I believe young Talbot is on the football team. He might know what happened to John."

"Is that where your son goes to school?"

"Yes. But he hasn't attended for at least a month, according to their records."

"Then he dropped out even before he disappeared."

"It would seem so."

"Alright, I'll start there."

It had all been very formal. Almost like he'd hired me to pick up his dry cleaning. For a guy whose son was missing, he seemed rather cold . . . stiff. Not that I would have expected a gush of emotion from an old bird like him, but he'd handled the entire transaction like he had a wooden stake up his ass.

15

"You'll keep me apprised of your progress?"

"Sure."

"That's a recent photo of him," said Prince, pointing one of his overly long fingernails at a framed photo on his desk.

He was a good-looking kid, slender like his father, with the same dark hair and eyes.

"You can take it with you if you like."

"Not necessary," I said. "I'm good with faces. I'll remember him."

More likely than not, the kid was playing backseat bingo with some dolly deep in Monster Town, with or without a needle in his arm. I'd roust some bums, ask a few questions, kick in the odd door or two, and probably find the little Prince in a few days . . . though, at a C-note a day, I might not be in any hurry.

Like I said, it wasn't show business, it was just a job . . . and that was jake with me.

2

GODZILLA BIG

I woke grudgingly to the harsh, grinding sound of garbage trucks and the sight of another dreary day outside my window. I closed my eyes and tried to ignore it all, but then the rain began with a crackling flash and a bang of clashing thunderclouds.

It had settled to a whimper of drizzle by the time I rolled out of bed. I hosed the porcelain and glanced in the mirror. Staring back at me was some ugly mug with a furrowed face, a heavily-stubbled jaw, and a Roman nose broken more times than the ancient aqueducts. I'd seen him somewhere before, but he didn't interest me much. So I gave him the cold shoulder, pulled on my trench coat, and grabbed my fedora.

By the time I got to *Maddie's Place*, another downpour had revved its dank engine. Rain dripped off the whitewashed eaves of the diner like a widow's tears.

Maddie's used to be a monster hangout. A friendly little cafe where the locals could meet and eat. These days, especially in the summer, it was usually filled with disappointed tourists, who didn't know it was their cameras and autograph books that drove the regulars away.

Fortunately for them, Madelina—or Maddie as she was known to most—was always happy to pose for a picture or two. I figured that's why she kept her signature silver screen beehive hairdo, complete with its bolts of gray. She was no dummy. She'd been the most famous bride in monster cinema, and she was working it for all the cups of coffee and grilled cheese sandwiches she could peddle.

Maddie's was close to my place, and I often stumbled in for my morning joe. It was the day after my trip to the Prince estate, but I wasn't that anxious to get to work. When I walked into the diner I saw Danny in his usual spot at the end of the counter. He was face-first in a plate of scrambled eggs and bacon.

17

"Hey, Danny boy. Katia's not cooking you breakfast today?"

He looked up at the sound of his name and I could see by the strands of bloodshot he hadn't slept much lately.

"We separated again, Dirk."

"That's too bad, Danny," I said unconvincingly.

Danny's wife wasn't my favorite person, and he knew it. She was a real witch—not that I have anything against witches. But when she got her broomstick out, you'd better duck. I tried to warn Danny before they got hitched, but love, whether it's true or comes out of a bottle, is a tough nut to crack. My theory, still unproven, was that she'd whipped together some love potion to get her hooks onto Danny's regular paycheck.

"You don't look so good this morning," I said. "That's usually my bailiwick."

"I'm on to a big story, Dirk. I mean Godzilla big."

Danny Legget was the star reporter for *The Daily Specter*, the local fish wrapper. He was good at what he did, honest, hardworking, a real truth-teller who pulled no punches. All of which had left him with few friends in town. I was one of them. We'd met years ago by chance, in a random foxhole on some godforsaken island in the South Pacific. He saved my life, I saved his, and we'd been pals ever since. In my four-plus decades in this world, he was probably the best friend I'd ever had.

"Tell me about this big story. Who you going to piss off this time?"

"Danny, you've got a call." Maddie pointed to the phone on wall she let her regulars use. Danny went for it like it was a dame in a negligee. Knowing Danny, though, I doubted the call had anything to do with a woman. Though, whatever it was, I could see his enthusiasm escalate as he spoke and scribbled sweet newshound nothings into his notebook.

"What'll it be this morning, Dirk?" asked Maddie.

"Just the usual."

"Coffee black and butter pecan ice cream?"

18

I nodded.

"You know that's not enough to keep those broad shoulders nourished," she said.

"Don't try to mother me, Maddie. I've already got one."

"Really? I could have sworn you were sewn together from various body parts."

"Very funny. Now go get my breakfast."

Danny hung up the phone, grabbed his homburg off the counter, and replaced it with a five-spot.

"Thanks, Maddie. I've got to run, Dirk."

"The Godzilla big story, I presume."

"Yeah. I got another tip. Wish I could tell you about it, but I've got to go. In the meantime, I'd advise you to start drinking your Scotch straight."

He shot out the door like a fullback headed for the end zone before I could ask him what the hell he meant by that crack. I didn't try. I knew better than to make a play for his attention when he was hot on the trail of a story.

Maddie brought me my joe and butter pecan.

"Boy, he was in a hurry," she said.

"Isn't he always?"

She chuckled and nodded.

"What's new with you, Maddie?"

"Same old hash-slinging—nothing exciting. Oh, there was some chrome dome in a fancy suit here the other day wanting to buy the place."

"Really? Was it a good offer?"

"I don't know. I guess so. But I ain't selling no ways. This place is all I got. It's all I know."

"Yeah, I'm with you on that. Though you have to wonder why someone would want this place—no offense."

"None taken. You're right. Most weeks I don't pull in that much. I'm thinking of making some changes though. Maybe with the decor.

I don't know. Maybe put up some old movie posters or other memorabilia. I've got some stashed in boxes somewhere."

"Well, I like it just fine the way it is."

She harrumphed—which I took to mean I'd drink my joe at the city dump if they let me.

"Hey, is your ex still the football coach down at the high school?"

"Frank? Yeah, he's still at Whale High."

"How's he doing?"

"Okay, as far as I know. Why do you ask?"

"I'm working a new case. I figure to ask him a few questions."

"Good luck with that. You might get in a couple questions in between wisecracks."

"Yeah, he's a real comedian . . . or thinks he is."

"You know what they say," she replied, wiping the counter. "One man's belly laugh is another's indigestion."

"What I want to know, is who are *they*?"

Maddie shrugged. "Whoever you want them to be I guess."

She sidled over to take another order and I got to work on my butter pecan. It was still raining frogs and alligators outside, so I was in no hurry.

3

THE HEEBIE-JEEBIES

Thunder continued to rap out a bossa nova beat far to the north, but the rain had broke for intermission over Monster Town when I pulled the Packard up to James Whale High School. Whale was an icon with the cinematic horror crowd, having directed the original *Frankenstein*, *The Invisible Man*, *The Bride of Frankenstein*, and *The Man in the Iron Mask*. So it was no surprise they'd named one of the local schools after him, or that Maddie's ex ended up coaching there.

Frank had been bad news not that long ago, working as muscle for some gangster. But he'd gone straight in an attempt to appease Maddie. That worked for about a week, as their relationship was as slippery as oil on ice. Maddie finally had all she could take, and threw Frank out on his overly large keister. Apparently the straight life stuck, and Frank ended up a phys ed teacher and coach.

I made my way to the football field, on the chance the team was working out. Once I found them, spotting Frank was easy. He was a good head higher than his tallest player, and it was a head that would have stood out in any crowd. His choice of a flattop military-style haircut might have been good for the tough-coach look, but it accentuated what wasn't his best feature.

He saw me coming and raised his hands in mock surrender. "Uh-oh, it's the heat. I surrender, Copper." He chortled at his own quip, his laugh sounding like a cross between a Clydesdale's snort and a hooker gagging on an oversized john.

He lowered his hands. "That's right, you're a private dick now, so I don't have to go quietly." He guffawed again, flashing his stained and uneven choppers. "Do you know what the mummy said to the detective?" When I didn't bite, he said, "Let's wrap this case up."

He was still laughing when I asked, "How you doing, Frank?"

"I'm not doing time, so that's a plus." He chuckled, then asked in a more serious tone, "You seen Madelina lately? How's she doing?"

"Maddie? Just saw her. She's doing fine."

"Good, good."

"I'm looking for a missing kid, Frank. Do you know a John Prince?"

He shook his massive noggin. "Doesn't spark any electrodes. Nobody by that name plays ball."

"I need to talk to one of your players—a friend of his—Harold Talbot."

"I don't know that I can let you do that, Slade. You're supposed to go through the administration to talk with any students. For all I know, you could be a corrupting influence." He laughed again.

"I just need a minute with him. Just a couple of questions to help me find this Prince kid."

He gave me his meanest monster stare, then broke out in a smile as big as . . . well as big as his enormous head.

"Alright, alright. Only cause I don't want you coming back here with torches and pitchforks."

I thought that was pretty funny, but he didn't laugh. He turned to where his players were warming up and called out, "Talbot! Front and center!"

I pulled out a smoke and lit up, waiting for the kid to hustle over. Frank turned, and when he saw me he went bat-shit crazy, waving his outstretched arms as if warding off evil and yelling, "Fire bad!"

I guess I was buying his act, because when he saw my startled expression he burst out in another asthmatic fit of laughter.

"I'm just messing with you," he said when he finally regained control. "That was a good one. The look on your face was priceless. But really, those things are bad for you. There's a reason they call them coffin nails. Speaking of things that will kill you, you know who this kid's father is, don't you?"

I hadn't really made the connection until he said that. Harold Talbot must be the son of Larry Talbot, or Frank wouldn't have said it that way. He was warning me I'd better watch my step.

"Coach Stein?"

Frank turned to his player and said, "Harry, this uh . . . gentleman has a few questions for you. You give him the straight scoop, okay?"

"Yes, Coach."

Once I got a closer look, I could see it was definitely a case of like father like son. He had dark-black, wiry hair where his uniform exposed his arms and lower legs. There was also some growing up like weeds around his neck. He wasn't tall, but he was well-muscled. I took him for a linebacker, and the rebellious scowl on his face when he spoke to me confirmed it.

"What do you want, mister?"

"I understand you're friends with a kid named John Prince."

"Yeah, so what?"

"I'm looking for him, that's what. Do you know where he is?"

"I haven't seen him."

"Do you know where he might have gone?"

The kid didn't look like he wanted to answer, but Frank was still standing nearby, flexing his menacing brow and staring at him with unhinged eyes. I guess the kid got the message.

"Last I saw him he'd joined the Fiends and was doing heeb."

I knew the Fiends were a local gang, but . . . "What's heeb?"

Frank chimed in, "Heeb, as in the heebie-jeebies. It's a new drug some of the kids are using. Bad stuff."

I'd heard of black birds, goofballs, jujus, gee, skid, skag, scorpion, snappers, snowbird, fall-down, and the white nurse, but I'd never heard of this heeb.

"I tried to talk him out of it," said young Harry. "I told him he was headed nowhere, that drugs were a dead end, but I think he just wanted to get back at his dad."

"Get back at him for what?"

He shrugged.

"Alright, kid. Thanks."

Frank nodded in the direction of the rest of the team, and the player took off running.

"Teenage boys and their fathers," said Frank, shaking his head. "What are you going to do with 'em, eh, Slade?"

"I wouldn't know."

"Well good luck finding the kid. Speaking of finding stuff, do you have any idea what you'd find between Godzilla's toes?"

I'd already turned and was walking away.

"Slow runners," called out Frank. "Get it? *Slow runners.*"

I left him in the midst of an uproarious spasm that surely scared small animals for miles around.

4

DEAD MEN WRITE NO COPY

Morning stretched her arms like a bright, cheery heroine, unaware a gruesome fate awaited her come sunset. My phone rang. I let it ring until my bruised hangover couldn't take it anymore. I crawled out of bed and answered it.

"Slade?"

"Yeah."

"You'd better get over here—Midtown, Browning Street, near the Water Department building."

Even only half awake, I recognized the voice. It was my ex-partner, Jimmy Halloran. I hadn't spoken to him in months. If he was calling, I knew it must be important. Still, I didn't like rude awakenings.

"Why don't you call my secretary and make an appointment."

He didn't say anything for a couple of beats. That's when I knew it was serious.

"It's Danny—Danny Legget," he said. "We found his body in an alley."

The sun exited stage left before I could even get to my car. The rain fell in sheets. It was pouring so hard my tattered wipers couldn't keep up. But I didn't let that slow me. I got to Midtown as fast as the Packard could grind it out. It wasn't fast enough for me. I was still grappling with what Halloran had said over the phone. I didn't doubt him, but I didn't want it to be true.

The deluge had eased up a little by the time I got there, but it was still coming down. As I pulled up I could see the usual ghouls hovering as close to the scene as the cops would let them rubberneck.

The alleyway was only partly sheltered, so I turned up the collar on my coat and limped across the street to where all the commotion was. I spotted Halloran, his customary three-piece suit drenched from the top down. There were crumbs scattered across his vest, but the bag of popcorn he usually carried hadn't survived the rain. I made my way towards him until a beat cop stopped me.

The uniform looked over. "Detective Halloran?"

"He's okay," said Halloran. "Let him through."

My eyes went right to the body on the ground. It was covered with a grubby varnish-stained tarp. I hesitated, but I had to see for myself. I bent down and pulled the tarp back. It was Danny alright.

"A couple of tourists found him," said Halloran, his gray trilby tilted back on his head as always. "He's still wearing his watch and wedding ring, but his wallet and keys are missing. I figure it was a mugging."

Muggers usually take watches and jewelry, but I figured whoever it was might have gotten spooked and took off.

"What else did he have on him?"

"Nothing. That was it."

"You didn't find a notebook?"

"No notebook."

"Danny always had his notebook on him," I said. "It was like a second skin. You ever hear of a mugger stealing a notebook, but leaving the jewelry?"

Halloran shrugged. "I've heard of all kinds of weird things."

Halloran was an honest cop, but not a particularly good one. He tended to take the easier path, pounce on the theory with the fewest dead ends. He didn't like to ruffle his feathers or anyone else's if he didn't have to.

"Maybe he pissed somebody off," said Halloran's new partner, stepping closer to Danny's body than I was comfortable with.

Groves was his name—Cliff Groves. I didn't know him very well, but I knew he was a real Neanderthal. And I don't say that just because he'd been in that one movie, *Neanderthal Man,* before he became a cop. That was pure typecasting, once the director did the math on his I.Q. Of course he thought his brief moment on the big screen made him special somehow.

"Every story he wrote about crime and corruption was a black eye on this city," said Groves. "Somebody was bound to take him out sooner or later."

I snatched Groves by his soggy lapels and lifted him just high enough to let him know I could. His perpetual glower melted in open-mouthed surprise, but his rancid breath almost knocked me for a loop.

It didn't matter that Groves might have been right about Danny pissing someone off. I didn't care for his attitude. He was a nitwit studying to be a dimwit so one day he could finally be a halfwit . . . and failing miserably.

"Let him go, Slade, or I'll have to run you in." Halloran put his hand on my shoulder.

I dropped him and he stumbled backwards. As soon as he had his footing, he pulled his gun out.

"You're under arrest, Slade," he snarled. "Assaulting a police officer."

Halloran stepped between us. "Put that heater away. You're not arresting anyone."

I could see Groves didn't want to back down, but he holstered the gat.

"Yeah, okay," he said, staring bullets at me. "I wouldn't want to shoot any innocent kids by mistake."

I wanted to take another run at him for that crack, but he'd hit me in the soft underbelly, so I just turned away so nobody could see my face.

"Take a walk, Cliff," ordered Halloran. "Get out of here."

I turned back to Danny. Old Doc Pretorius, the coroner, had arrived and was checking the body. I'd worked with the doc many times in the old days.

"See the bruising around the neck?" he said, showing me. "It's just a preliminary exam, but I'd say he was strangled by someone with very large hands. Even larger than those twin meat hooks of yours, Slade."

"Probably some monster," said Halloran.

"How do you know it was a monster?" I asked, even though I was thinking the same thing.

"Isn't it always in this town?"

Halloran gave the order to move the body and clear the scene, and I was about to drift. I wanted to go to Danny's place — the one he used for writing . . . and for when he and Katia weren't getting along — which was most of the time. I had to find Danny's notebook. If it wasn't on him, and wasn't taken by the killer, it should be in his apartment. I wasn't buying the happenstance of a mugging theory. I was hoping the notebook might have a clue as to what happened to him.

Before I could leave, I heard something. There was a pile of old boxes and other trash strewn along the alley. The sound was coming from there. It was kind of a mewling. For all I knew, some street kid might be under all that trying to keep dry. Maybe there was a witness the cops hadn't found.

I moved a couple of pieces of waterlogged cardboard before I discovered the witness. It was a scrawny little black cat, soaked to the tip of its ragged ears.

"Hey, Alley Cat. You didn't happen to see a murder last night did you?"

The pitiful thing mewed at me.

"I didn't think so." I picked it up by the scruff of the neck, held it out, and looked at it. *Pitiful* was being generous. "You'd better come along with me in case your memory improves."

I dried her the best I could with a rag I had in the Packard, and headed for Danny's place.

5

MCGUFFIN, MCGUFFIN, WHO'S GOT THE MCGUFFIN?

The dreary sky finally ran out of ammunition and called a halt to its wretched barrage by the time I arrived at Danny's. I left Alley Cat in the Packard and headed upstairs, pondering, as I huffed and puffed, why no one in Monster Town believed in elevators.

I wasn't sure how I'd get in. There was always the landlord or my big right foot.

Turned out it didn't matter. The door was ajar. I didn't hear anything from inside, but decided caution was the better part of valor. I reached for my piece out of pure reflex. A sharp stab of recollection and a wave of anguish reminded me why I didn't carry anymore. The fleeting pain in my head was real, even if the cause was a figment. I mustered my wits and slowly pushed the door open.

I heard nothing . . . saw nothing, except that the place had been thoroughly ransacked. One look told me I wouldn't find Danny's notebook, but I searched anyway. Either someone had found it here or on Danny's body after they killed him. What was clear to me now, was that it had been no random mugging that had led to Danny's death. He was targeted. And there was no question in my mind that the hit was related to something he'd written . . . or something he was going to write.

There was no sign of the notebook, or anything else I could relate to the "big story" Danny had mentioned. Maybe his editor would know what he was working on.

As I searched, something caught my eye. It was just a glint of light reflecting off the floor, but it stood out among the scattered debris that now decorated Danny's place. I bent down and picked it up. It was a jet-black matchbook embossed with silver lettering that read *Sanctuary*.

I knew the place. It was a nightclub frequented by the real denizens of Monster Town—not a tourist trap. It was a gloomy, smoky hideaway that survived on the patronage of has-beens, ne'er-do-wells, pickpockets, scam artists, and some of the ugliest mugs you would ever lay your eyes on. I used to go there quite a bit myself, until I took a liking to a more intimate setting for two—just me and my bottle.

I wondered about the matchbook. Contrary to every hackneyed hard-bitten reporter I'd ever seen in the movies, Danny didn't smoke. I opened it. It was full of matches and something else. There was something written there, in Danny's handwriting. Just one word. A name. *Janice.*

Before I could wonder if I knew any Janices, I heard a noise out in the hallway. I hurried over as fast as my hobbled leg could take me, and pressed myself flat against the wall next to the door. If the killer was coming back for another look, I'd grab him before he knew I was there.

Turned out it was no killer. It was Danny's editor at the *Specter*, Fritz Igor. I'd only met him a couple of times, but each time he was decked out as he was now, in a big panama and a white linen suit.

He stepped into the room and froze, staring at the mess. He saw me out of the corner of his eye and almost retreated in panic. Then he recognized me and threw his hand to his chest as if he were calming his heart.

"Hello, Fritz."

"Mr. Slade, you scared the dickens out of me. The police called me about Danny, and I've been on edge ever since." He motioned to the clutter. "I take it you didn't do this."

I shook my head. "Somebody was looking for something. I figure it was Danny's notebook. The police say they didn't find it on his body."

"I can't believe he would have left it here," said Igor, taking off his hat and fanning himself with it. "He always carried it with him. He'd go out naked before he'd leave his notebook."

"Yeah, that was Danny. Just the same, I searched the place. I didn't find it, or anything else that would tell me who did this. Yesterday Danny told me he was working on some big story — 'Godzilla big' was the way he put it. But he didn't have time to fill me in before he was off chasing it. Do you know what he was on the trail of?"

"No, Danny had a habit of keeping everything pretty close to the vest until he had all the facts. He was a good reporter, so I always let him be until he was ready. He never let me down."

The Daily Specter wasn't a big paper, but it never pulled any punches. Danny was always saying how Igor let him run with a story no matter where it took him. This time it took him to the morgue, by way of a dark damp alley under a shabby length of old tarp.

"I don't know what he was working on this time," said Igor. "But he mentioned in an offhand way something about a Pulitzer. I thought he was joking."

"Would he have been working on anything that had to do with Scotch?"

"Scotch? The drink?" He looked at me queerly.

"It was just something he said to me. It was probably just Danny playing with words as usual."

"You know," said Igor, "his death might not have had anything to do with what he was working on. He and the paper have made a lot of enemies regarding stories already published."

He was right. The list of possible suspects would be as long as a bad musical if you included everyone Danny ever wrote about and probably pissed off, including, if my memory wasn't too whisky-bitten, my current employer, Vladimir Prince. I seemed to recall something Danny wrote sometime back about one of his businesses that wasn't very flattering. But that was years ago. It wouldn't make any sense to be connected now.

"I saw your old friend Frank Stein down at the high school the other day."

"We were never really friends," said Igor, taking off his specs and cleaning them with his tie. "Just coworkers. I didn't care for the way he always tried to bully me."

"Well, he just got me to thinking. Have you heard from your old on-screen employer recently?"

"Old Doc Frankenstein? No, I haven't. Why do you ask?"

"I know he lost his medical license because of a story Danny did on him."

"And you think that makes him a suspect?"

I nodded.

"I seriously doubt it. He's not up to it—physically or mentally. Last I heard he was doing hair transplants in a little shop down on Boo Street, while dealing with a bad case of rheumatism. I don't think he's your man."

"You're probably right." I mulled it over. There were just too many possible suspects to start throwing darts. I needed facts. "On an unrelated subject, what do you know about the Fiends?"

"The gang? I know they've been very active lately. Taking turf from other gangs, vandalism, dealing drugs, even a few murders that have been attributed to them but not proven."

"What's this drug heeb I heard about?"

"Dangerous stuff," said Igor. "It's like a cross between heroin and mescaline. We've had several reports of fatal overdoses already. It's monstrous."

"The perfect drug for an imperfect town."

6

BITCH OF A WITCH

I dropped Alley Cat off at my place, then grabbed a burger and a belt, so it was late in the day by the time I got to Katia's place. I switched off the ignition, but I didn't get right out. I sat in the Packard for a minute and brooded. The rain had left its mark, both on me and on the city. Puddled shadows adorned every crack and crevice along the litter-strewn road. Curbside garbage cans glistened with anticipation, and foul steam wafted through a nearby sewer grate, no doubt leading rodent families to intense squabbles about relocation.

I didn't want to go see Danny's widow. We'd never gotten along. But I figured I needed to cover all my bases—see if she knew anything about what Danny was working on. I wasn't positive, yet my gut was still raging with suspicion, telling me Danny's murder wasn't a random act—that Halloran was wrong. The truth is, I didn't trust my own cynicism.

As I got out of the car, pages of *The Daily Specter* blew by me like portentous tumbleweeds. I couldn't help but feel that Danny's ghost was right behind me. I even turned to look. It wasn't a ghost at all. It was something else—*someone* else. Someone who'd blown in with the breeze and a burst of fairy dust. It was Kink.

"Hiya, Bud."

"What'cha know, Kink?"

"Same old shit," she responded, fluttering her wings and adjusting her altitude until all six inches of her were eye level with me. "I was sorry to hear about Danny though. He was good people—a real human being."

"Yeah, he was."

"I don't have to ask to know you're going to find the scum who did it."

33

"That's right. I'm still looking for leads. Going up to see Katia now."

"The witch?"

I nodded.

"You need backup?" Her little fairy eyes sparkled with earnestness.

"Sure. It's always good to have you along, Kink."

She dove like an Olympian, managed a full barrel roll with great finesse, and soared up behind my right ear, landing on my shoulder.

"Let's go, partner," she said resolutely.

Kink hadn't always been Kink. A few years back she'd been *Wink*, the newest, brightest, animated character bound for a series of kiddie flicks. The first film opened with great success, at least until she was photographed in a compromising position with an old gnome and a prepubescent pixie. The photo started making the rounds, finally hitting the front pages of the trades. The studio couldn't pull the movie from circulation fast enough. I heard they even burned the original prints.

Needless to say, they voided her contract on a little-used morals clause and bounced her pert little ass to the curb—wings and all. She went from an overnight success to a pariah. No longer welcome in La-La Land, she exiled herself to Monster Town.

It wasn't long before everyone knew her sad and kinky backstory. No one cared. She fit right in. But everyone started calling her Kink instead of Wink, and the name stuck.

Both being outcasts of a sort, we became friends right off the bat. Yet, despite her renewed debauchery and our occasional sexual banter, we were strictly platonic. Kink was like my little sister. My very little, high-strung, lascivious sister.

I knocked on Katia's door. It wasn't two shakes of a rattler's tail before it opened. Standing there was this brute of a guy so big he dwarfed me. He was bald as a brick and almost the same color. His slack-jawed, gap-toothed, indistinct countenance gave him that not-quite-complete look. It took me a moment to realize he was a straight-up golem. Hell, he still had clay residue on his clothes.

He didn't say a word, just opened the door wide enough for me to see Katia lounging on her sofa. She didn't look at all like your stereotypical witch. She was slim, blonde, a real looker—more Glinda than Wicked Witch of the West. She could almost be described as beautiful, except for the metaphorical wart on her nose that was her personality.

"Hello, Dirk," she said as casual as could be. Then she saw Kink. "Hello, *Kink*. Fellate any gnomes lately?" Her acknowledgement of my fairy friend was as cordial as a glacier. I was told the bad blood between them went back to some incident related to an enchanted dragonfly and an ancient curse, but I wasn't privy to the details.

"Hello, *Katia*." Kink's response was just as icy, though at the *K* sound she kind of spit in my ear. "Still eating eye of newt for dinner, or do you save that for dessert now?"

The golem growled, though I wasn't sure if it came from his throat or his stomach.

"I wanted to pay my respects and tell you how sorry I am about Danny," I said, taking off my hat and trying to interject a little civility. "Whatever I can do, just let me—"

"You can tell the insurance company to get off its fiduciary ass and pay off Danny's policy," she said matter-of-factly. "That would be a big help."

For a day-old widow, she wasn't that broken up. But she'd always been a real bitch of a witch. I decided there was a limit to my cordiality.

"Who's this?" I asked, nodding at the hunk of pottery holding the door.

"My brother, Paul. Say hello to our guests, Paul."

" . . . 'lo," he mumbled as if it were a struggle to get even a fraction of the word out.

She called him her brother, but I wasn't buying it. I don't ever remember her mentioning a brother. If he was, then that made the vibe I was getting from the two of them more than a little incestuous.

35

Which made the next thing she said even more outrageous.

"Don't look so high and mighty, Mr. Private Dick," she declared, either reading my face or my mind. "I know Danny was having an affair. He was shacked-up with some dolly somewhere, I'm sure of it."

I took a deep breath . . . and wished I hadn't. The room stunk of wet dirt and rancid petroleum jelly.

"Katia, I can guarantee you Danny wasn't having an affair. He was too caught up in his work to even think about some dame. The only thing he had his arms wrapped around was a hot new story."

She jumped off the sofa, her cool façade disintegrating for the first time.

"He was always too wrapped up with some hot new story!" she practically screamed. "He loved his damn stories more than he loved me."

It wasn't just Katia who was upset. At the moment of her outburst, her "brother" seemed to come alive with anger. And I was the focus of that anger. He came at me with fire in his eyes, grabbed my trench coat, and yanked me into his face. His breath smelled of dust and blackberry douche.

"Paul! Put him down," commanded Katia.

By this time, Kink was buzzing around the golem's head like a swarm of angry bees. He let go of me and swatted at her. But he was mud and she was lightning.

"Better call off your lawn ornament, bitch," warned Kink, "or I'll pulverize him."

Kink had a hell of a temper for someone with a five-inch wingspan. And when it came to drama, she was cooking with helium. I guess some old habits are tough to kick.

"Paul, sit down."

Paul obeyed, and Katia sat back on the sofa with him, stroking his adobe head as if to calm him.

I don't like to be manhandled, so I was plenty frosted. But I didn't lose my composure. I just peeled off a couple of layers of fabricated charm.

"Okay, okay. I know you and Danny weren't the lovebirds you once were. But I'm going to find out who killed him, no matter how long it takes, or where I have to look."

A concerned expression took shape on her face.

"Don't look at me," she said.

The funny thing is, I hadn't been looking at her . . . until she said that. Then it hit me like the brick she was fondling. Maybe she brewed up brother Paul with the idea of cashing in on Danny's life insurance policy. Doc Pretorius said Danny looked like he'd been strangled by someone with extremely large hands. The golem's mitts certainly fit the bill. Or maybe she really thought Danny was having an affair, and had him killed in a fit of jealous witch rage.

I decided to convince her I *wasn't* looking at her for the murder.

"I think maybe Danny's death had to do with a story he was working on. You have any idea what it was?"

"He never told me what he was working on. He always kept it to himself."

I knew that was a lie. Danny often told me how he tried to tell her about his work, but that she had no interest in it. It "bored her" was how he put it.

"Do you have any idea where Danny's notebook is?"

"That? He always carried it with him," she said, moving her hand from the golem's brow to his thigh. "He acted like that notebook was made of gold or something."

"What about you, Paul? Danny ever talk to you about what he was working on?"

"No."

"By the way, what kind of work do you do?"

The golem looked at me with those dead rheumy eyes of his and said clearly, without muttering, "I'm a Sunday school teacher. What's it to you?"

So old terra-cotta head *could* talk. And, based on the loam rising up in his kiln, he could get excited too.

I had no desire to see any clay on witch action, so I said, "Let's go, Kink."

"Danny's dead, Dirk," said Katia. "It won't do any good to stir up things now. Let him rest."

You'd think, no matter how bad things had gotten between them, that if she ever cared for Danny she'd want to know who killed him. Unless . . . .

I put my fedora back on, and replied, "He's not dead until we forget him."

I turned and walked out, but not before I saw Kink give the golem the one-gun salute. What I can say? She wasn't exactly a sugar plum fairy.

As soon as we were out of earshot, she asked, "Do you think they did it?"

"Did what?"

"Come on, Dirk. You're thinking the same thing I am. The witch and her lumpy new squeeze killed Danny for the insurance money."

"Maybe."

"I got that as a two-to-one maybe in my book," said Kink. "Well, I gotta blow. It's been fun."

An invisible bell tinkled lightly somewhere, and Kink, as she was prone to do without notice or niceties, vanished in a sparkle of fairy dust, leaving behind only a sensuous swirl of white smoke.

7

WHAT'S A NICE GIRL LIKE YOU . . .

Night crept over the city like it was slithering out of the grave. The storm had moved on and there was a stillness in the air that wasn't altogether natural. But I was in Monster Town, and strange was always on the menu.

I had only one clue to pursue—the nightclub matchbook I found in Danny's apartment with the name Janice written in it. So I put on my best drinking duds and headed for the *Sanctuary*. It was nearby, so I decided to give my bum leg a workout and go for a walk.

You didn't walk alone at night in this part of town, so I lit a smoke to keep me company. As I made my way down the sidewalk, I made a point of flexing my powers of observation. It might have been my mood at the time, but every awning, every windowpane seemed alive. Every measure of gloom had its own eerie anecdote. Heavy shadows, burdened by past narratives of crime and passion, lurked at every corner. Cracks in the pavement were great chasms of disillusionment. Garbage bins provoked wariness, and across the dull night sky, rooftop neon fluttered like a doxy's eyelashes.

Outside the *Sanctuary,* a zombie mime was working the street. He was no Marcel Marceau, but he had talent. I dropped four bits in his hat and felt a twinge in my leg. Apparently even a short walk was too much for me these days. I limped up to the front door where an ogre I didn't recognize was working as the bouncer. He eyed me but didn't say a thing. I went inside and was immediately assaulted by an array of sights, sounds, and smells. The band was loud, the customers almost as noisy, and the place reeked of sweat and booze.

The joint was packed, so it was slow-going to reach the bar. On my way I spotted several familiar faces—most as repugnant as a hobgoblin's belly button. One of the mugs belonged to Larry Talbot,

Boss Wolf, the biggest, meanest gangster in Monster Town, and father of the kid I'd talked to. He was holding forth in a corner booth with a pack of his cronies, each uglier than the next. There was also a dame with him—one I didn't recognize. She'd been poured into a silver lamé dress, but it couldn't contain all of her. Fortunately, the parts popping out were pleasingly round and soft. Even at 50 feet she was a real knockout.

I only glanced at her, but she gave me the eye. Whether it was the evil eye or she was flirting, I didn't care to find out. You didn't mess with Boss Wolf's property. He was a guy you didn't want to cross, on or off screen. If he wasn't in the mood to tear you apart himself, he had plenty of soldiers with gruesome techniques all their own.

I was familiar with the band that was playing—Sonny D and the Night Dogs. They played a nice variety of tunes. Their leader, a.k.a. the Hideous Sun Demon, a.k.a. Gil McKenna, was a guy I'd helped out of a jam some time back. He sang a little and played guitar. Backing him up was the Mad Ghoul on sax, the Mummy on skins, a troll on stand-up bass, some icy-looking creature on trumpet, and a guy I didn't know on the bones.

When I finally reached the bar I found a seat. Before I could say a word I had a Scotch-rocks in front of me.

"Hi, Quasi. How's business?"

The hunchback bartender gestured at the packed house and didn't bother to answer. Instead he replied, "How's the P.I. game? You gonna be able to pay for that drink?"

"I'm flush, Quasi. I can even pay my tab—whatever that might be."

He aimed his glassy eye at me with a look like he'd believe that when he saw it, and moved on down the bar.

Quasimodo wasn't just the bartender, he was, for as long as I could remember, the owner of the *Sanctuary*. I counted him among the few friends I had in Monster Town, though we didn't really hang out. Quasi pitched for the other team, so mostly I just saw him when I came in for a drink.

"Who's the new piano man?" I asked when he came by again.

"Paul Orlac's his name."

"What happened to the Phantom of the Opera guy?"

"The new owners didn't like him living in the attic. They kicked him out," said Quasi, pouring a couple of beers. "I think he's playing the organ over at the ballpark now."

"New owners? You didn't sell the bar, did you?"

"Had to. I just couldn't keep up with the taxes and insurance and . . . ." He made a circular on-and-on motion with his hand.

"I'm sorry to hear that, Quasi."

"It's okay. They gave me a sweet deal. The number was hard to turn down. It gives me plenty for retirement, and they put me on salary. Said I could keep working here, keep running the place until they decided what to do with it."

"They're not going to close down the *Sanctuary*, are they?"

He just shrugged and moved on down the bar with his tray of beers.

I couldn't imagine the place being closed. Where would all the miscreants go then? The *Sanctuary* was an icon, a monument to bestial depravity, a shrine to wild, fiendish mayhem. It would be a sad day if it was closed down. People would not be happy. Monsters would be angry.

I looked around and eventually spotted Kink. She was oscillating over a booth where Frank Stein and a couple of the Alligator People were hanging out. When she saw me she flew right over.

"Hey, Bud. How's it hanging?" she asked, doing a midair pirouette. It wasn't her best, so I could tell she'd been drinking. Still, fairies have a high tolerance. I'd never seen her so drunk she couldn't fly, though there were many times I had to be her navigator.

"It's hanging," I responded.

Kink was decked out in a revealing bustier, some hot little shorts, and sheer nylons that disappeared invitingly into those shorts. With that flame-top hair of hers, she was ready to scorch someone good.

Don't doubt for a moment she was woman enough to make the
Pope question his religion . . . especially if the Pope were only six
inches.

Not that you had to be her size. She could do things with her wings
that would make a man howl like a possessed demon. Not that I
would know firsthand. Like I said before, Kink and I were just friends,
though we often cracked-wise about the day that would change.

Quasi walked over to his little bell and began pulling the string that
made it ring, as he was wont to do when he got a large tip. "Sanctuary!
Sanctuary!" he called out.

"Hey, Kink," said Quasi. "You need anything?"

Kink shook her head but asked, "You want to hear a joke?"

"Too busy right now," said Quasi. "Tell Slade."

"You've been hanging out with Frank, haven't you?"

"Brilliant detective work, Bud. So . . . What did the mommy ghost
say to the baby ghost?" She waited, even though she knew I wouldn't
answer. "Don't spook until you're spoken to."

That cracked her up. She flew a couple of inside loops, laughing the
whole time. I had to admit, it *was* kind of funny.

She landed on the bar and tossed me another one. "Why don't
mummies take vacations? They're afraid they'll relax and unwind."

That had her rolling around with the giggles until she hit a wet
spot. She came up cursing like a mechanic, and fluttering her wings at
high speed to dry off.

At that moment, Talbot's woman decided to stretch her legs. They
were quite a pair of gams, and by the way she strolled over to the bar,
she knew it. As she neared me, I got a better look.

Across the room she looked like a lot of class, but up close she
looked like someone made up to be seen from across the room. There
was a hard, used look about her, though she seemed durable. With
Boss Wolf as her man, she'd need to be.

"Haven't seen you in here before," she said, practically purring.

"Haven't been here in a while," I replied, trying not to hear the siren's call of her cleavage.

By that time, Kink was hovering between us like a winged prophylactic. She wasn't smiling.

"Who's your little friend?" asked the dame.

"His *little* friend is big enough to—"

I interrupted what was sure to be one of Kink's more colorful assertions. "This is Kink. I'm Dirk. And you are . . . ?"

"June's the name."

"Are you lost, June? Would you like me to escort you back over to your large hairy friend across the way?" When I nodded in the direction she'd come from, I saw Talbot on his way over. "Speaking of Sasquatch," I said, turning back to my drink.

"What are you doing over here?" Talbot had a voice like hot gravel. I remembered it from my days on the beat.

"Just stretching my legs, Wolf."

"Well get your big ass back to the table," he growled.

I thought her posterior was the perfect size, but I kept my mouth shut for once.

"You can stretch your legs when we get home . . . around my neck."

I found his second comment a tad crude, and this time I just couldn't let it slide.

"Always the perfect gentleman, eh, Talbot?"

He looked at me under those bushy beetle brows of his as if seeing me for the first time. He sniffed the air. It seemed to take him a couple of ticks to identify me. When he did, he exhaled a quick sardonic laugh.

"That you, Slade? Didn't recognize you off your knees. Shoot any kids lately?"

I wanted to pretend I didn't hear him, and I wanted to pop him at the same time. I froze and couldn't do either.

He turned to follow his woman and I had to pluck Kink out of the air. She was going after him.

"That lousy fur ball," she spat. "I'll pull the hairs out of his hide one by one."

"Easy, Kink. Nobody wants to see a bald werewolf."

That cracked her up again. When she stopped laughing, she said seriously, "You'd better stay away from that Jezebel, Bud. She's big trouble."

"Who is she?"

"That's Leech Woman. Ever seen the flick?"

"Can't say I have."

"Well she uses men up and tosses them out like so much stale bread."

"Don't worry, Kink. I'll give that one a wide berth. Hey, I meant to ask you the other day. Do you know where the Fiends hang out?"

"The local juvenile delinquents? Mostly they hang in and around the community pool. Why?"

"Just another case I'm working on."

"Alright, Bud, I gotta fly. But just one more joke before I go."

"Another one of Frank's?"

"Who else? What do you get when you cross a vampire and a snowman?"

"Frostbite," I said before she could.

"Bastard. You've heard that one. Alright, check you later. Gotta get back to my gators."

Wham, bam, and she'd scrammed, leaving her telltale eddy of fairy dust and pearly smoke. I glanced over to where Frank and his alligator friends were sitting. Sure enough, Kink was already doing her fairy thing over there.

I lifted my Scotch and took a drink. For no particular reason, I looked into my glass and recalled what Danny had said to me. *Start drinking your Scotch straight.* Was it a joke? A warning? I stared at the ice cubes floating in there like they were going to get up and do a dance. I pulled out the matchbook I'd found at Danny's place.

"Do you know a Janice that comes in here, Quasi?"

"Janice?" He thought about it a second or two. "Oh, you mean Star."

"Star?"

"Janice Starlin is her real name. Star's her stage name."

"Do you know where I can find her?"

Quasi hooked his thumb over his shoulder toward the band. "She's just about to go on."

I looked but couldn't see who he was talking about.

"She's with the band?"

"She's not really a regular member, but they're always asking her to come up and sing with them, so I hired her part-time. She's good."

I looked again. She was just walking up to the mike. She was good indeed. Dressed in a slinky black number ringed with silver, she had the tiniest waist I'd ever seen—which only served to magnify her other lovely attributes. With bird-bright eyes and raven hair that fell past her shoulders, she was a real dish. One I could imagine myself getting a taste of. And she could sing.

She started off with "That Ol' Black Magic," and when she sang *"The same old witchcraft when your eyes meet mine"* I could have sworn she was looking straight at me. Of course, a dozen other guys in the place were probably thinking the same thing. She was spellbinding.

I snapped myself out of it and thought about the matchbook. Why would Danny have just written her name—no phone number, no address, nothing else? Why didn't he write Star? How did he know her name was Janice? What was their connection?

I didn't believe for a moment that Danny had some kind of affair going with this doll. That wasn't Danny. Besides, she looked like a full-time job, and Danny already had one.

I didn't know how long that matchbook had been on his floor. Maybe he'd interviewed her for a story some time back. She likely had nothing at all to do with his murder—or with whatever he'd been working on.

She finished to rousing applause and went right into "I'll Never Smile Again." In sync with the lyrics, her captivating almond eyes took on a sadness that seemed all too real. When she sang *"I'll never love again,"* I was convinced she wouldn't. I wondered who it was she loved before, and what the hell the crumb had done to her.

At the last line, *"until I smile at you,"* she tried to smile, but I could see it was forced. She bowed her head, the applause rang out again, and she moved quickly off stage.

"Let's hear it for Star!" called out Sonny D, extending the applause with his own. "Star!"

I watched her go to a table in the back. I didn't hesitate. I got up and made my way over. She was busy looking in her purse and didn't even see me standing there, hat in hand, so I said, "You're very good. You've got a great set of pipes."

She glanced up at me like I was nothing but a mote in her line of vision. It was such a look of disinterest it would have gutted a lesser man.

She didn't say a thing. She made me stand there like some chucklehead for a couple of drawn out seconds.

"Is that some sort of childish innuendo?" she finally asked, her eyelashes quivering like the antennae of some angry insect.

"No, I mean it. You've got a great voice. Too good for this place."

She looked up at me again like she was checking to see if I was serious or putting her on. If there was any sadness in her eyes, you couldn't see it behind the aloof sparks that blazed there now.

"Can I sit down?" I asked, sitting before she could answer. "Would you like a drink?" I motioned for the waitress.

"You're a take charge kind of guy, aren't you?"

"When I have to be."

"What if I don't want you to sit? What if I don't want a drink?"

"Then I'll leave you alone. I just need to ask you a couple of questions first."

"Are you a cop?"

"Not any more. My name's Dirk—Dirk Slade. I'm a private investigator."

That seemed to tickle her interest.

"What kind of questions did you want to ask me, Mr. Slade?"

A waitress I knew, Esmeralda, stepped up and asked, "What'll it be, Slade?"

"A Scotch-rocks for me."

"What do you want, honey?" asked Esmeralda.

"A virgin margarita."

I didn't see Esmeralda walk away, because I was staring at Star. It wasn't hard. Long lashes, full lips, high cheekbones, delicate features . . . she was gorgeous—a real stunner. I caught my jaw before it dropped.

"So, what were you going to ask me? What's a nice girl like me doing in a place like this?"

"Maybe later," I said. "First I wanted to ask how you knew Danny Legget."

"Legget? That doesn't ring any bells."

She plucked a smoke out of her purse, but before she could find a light, I pulled out the matchbook and struck one up. She leaned in and I lit it for her.

"I found your name on this matchbook in Danny's apartment." I flipped it open and showed her. "So I figured you might have spoken with him."

She exhaled a stream of smoke through those luscious lips of her, and my imagination began to heat.

"Not many people know my real name," she said. "What kind of racket is this Danny in?"

"He was a reporter."

"Oh yeah, I remember him now. The reporter. He was in here a couple of times asking questions . . . like you. Why'd you say he *was* a reporter?"

"He's dead."

"Oh, I didn't know." She took another drag. "I just got back into town. I was in Hollywood for an audition."

I could see she was holding something back, but I believed her

47

when she said she didn't know Danny was dead.

"I'm sorry to hear about that. I didn't really know him, but he seemed nice. Was he a friend of yours?"

"Yeah. A good friend."

"Good friends are rare," she said wistfully, looking away. "How did he die?"

"He was murdered."

"Oh."

I didn't know if that surprised her or not. Her reaction wasn't typical, but I was having a hard time getting a read on her. Or maybe it wasn't her at all. Maybe it was me, sitting there drooling. I couldn't really help myself. She was hot enough to burst into flames, but she just sat there, smoking.

"You have any idea who might have killed him?" I said quickly, trying to provoke a more impulsive response. It didn't work.

"What kind of question is that?" she asked, unruffled.

"A yes-or-no one."

"The answer's *no*. How would I know who killed him?"

She blew smoke and a razor-edged glance in my direction.

"No reason I know of. Thought I'd ask." I lit my own, took a drag, exhaled, and stared right back at her. "I'm going to find his killer, and I'm going to take him down—one way or the other."

"I hope you do," she said without emotion.

"Then you wouldn't mind telling me what kinds of questions Danny asked you."

"I said he was in here asking questions. I didn't say he asked *me* any."

She was sharp, and she was paying attention. But she wasn't being very helpful. I wondered why.

"You must have talked with him about something . . . or heard him talk about something."

She hesitated again, then seemed to reach some inner decision.

"I did hear him talking about the Water Department once. He

mentioned how he was going to interview the guy who runs the show there. The manager or something—a Mr. Jekyll or Dr. Jekyll. That's all I recall. I don't know what it was all about."

I thought about it. Danny was a crime reporter. Why would he care about the Water Department? There could be a criminal connection but . . . then I remembered. Danny's body was found just down the street from the city water works. Coincidence? Maybe. But once again I heard his last words to me. *Start drinking your Scotch straight.*

"You wouldn't happen to know anything about Danny's notebook, would you?"

She shrugged. "I know he had one. I saw him writing in it. Why?"

"It's missing. I'm looking for it."

"You think it has a clue to who killed him?"

"Possibly." I wasn't sure why she was acting so inscrutable, but I didn't think she knew anything about Danny's killing. The question was, what was she hiding? "Well, I appreciate you taking the time to answer my questions."

"Sorry I couldn't be more helpful."

We both took a drink. She looked at me and when I looked back, she glanced away and took another drag of her smoke.

"So, what *is* a nice girl like you doing in a place like this?"

She laughed. It was the first crack in her icy façade I'd seen.

"Do you mean why am I singing in the *Sanctuary*?"

"Not so much that. This place isn't that bad. I guess I'm asking what brought you to Monster Town."

"Oh, you know, the usual. The dreams of a small-town girl who wanted to become a leading lady."

"And . . . ?"

She looked wistful again. "I learned the stuff that dreams are made of eventually crumble and are swept away into life's dirty dustpan."

"That dustpan being Monster Town."

She nodded, took another drag, and then rubbed the butt into an ashtray.

"And yet you're still out there trying," I said, "still auditioning."

Her face grew serious, her eyes teary, she looked slightly upward and declared with just the right accent, "After all, tomorrow is another day." It was a pretty good Scarlett O'Hara. Vivien Leigh would have been impressed.

"I get it. But why Monster Town? You don't look the part."

"I don't look like a monster? Why how kind of you, Mr. Slade."

"You know what I mean."

"Yes, but I *was* a monster. That was my big chance. My one opportunity. When it came knocking, I was ready. I even played the title role. Did you ever see *Wasp Woman*?"

I had seen it. I didn't remember it that well, but I didn't want to tell her that.

"I don't think I did."

"Well, that's me—Wasp Woman." She stood up and posed with her arms outstretched, her palms up. "Ta-da!"

She quickly sat back down.

"That was my big break," she said. "Or at least I thought it was. The movie bombed, and blew up my budding career with it."

She took a sip of her drink and looked melancholy.

I tried to remember the movie. I couldn't place her, but I recalled it was about a woman who, trying desperately to regain her youth, injected herself with an experimental formula made from the royal jelly of a wasp queen. It made her young again, but it also made her a murderous killer. I wondered how much of the storyline was her, and how much was scripted.

"Did you ever see the movie *Leave Her to Heaven*?"

"I don't think so."

"You're not much of a movie guy, are you?"

Actually, I saw a lot of movies, but I just shrugged and responded, "Why do you ask?"

"Gene Tierney plays a killer in the movie, and one of her victims is named Danny. That's why I thought of it."

"Yeah, so?"

"So how do you know it was a man that killed him—killed your friend, Danny?"

"What do you mean?"

"Earlier you said, 'I'm going to find his killer, and I'm going to take him down.' What makes you so sure it was a him and not a her?"

I thought about it. Sure, Doc Pretorius said he'd been strangled by very large hands. But those hands could have been directed by a *her*. By Katia or . . . ?

"You're right. I'm *not* sure."

8

GRAVESIDE MANNER

I realized the next day that I'd gained a roommate—at least on a temporary basis. Alley Cat had apparently taken a liking to my tiny apartment, even though I left a window open for her to take a powder whenever she wanted. So I got her a litter box, some bowls for food and water, and generally tried to make her feel welcome in my lap . . . at least for as long as I could sit still. It wasn't long. I had two cases on my plate, and barely an hors d'oeuvres worth of leads.

Without warning, the lamp on my end table toppled, crashing on the floor. I tossed Alley Cat from my lap to the sofa and was on my feet in a blink. Just as quickly I saw the sheer curtains fluttering like crazy and realized with a healthy amount of chagrin what it was. I don't know why I was so jumpy. I chastised myself with a few unkind words about my age and looked out the window. The winds were whipping up like the Furies themselves were coming to pay me a visit. I closed it tight.

My next order of business was to call Igor at *The Daily Specter* and find out what I could about this Jekyll character Star had mentioned. It turned out, though it was no surprise, he was *the* Dr. Jekyll of cinematic fame. Of course, as the singer made clear about herself, one film doesn't make you a star . . . unless that's what you change your name to. So Jekyll had found work outside the movies.

As for Star, I didn't know what to make of her. I didn't know how she fit into my investigation, or *if* she fit. But I couldn't get her out of my head. Whether it was because she'd been less than forthcoming or something more primal, I wasn't sure. Okay, that wasn't exactly true. I knew she had my engine overheating from the moment I laid eyes on her. I just didn't know if I should try to do anything about it. So I threw myself into my work.

Igor told me Dr. Henry Jekyll had been the director of the local water department for eight years now. Which meant he was an entrenched bureaucrat, probably miserable in his job, likely open to new opportunities. Igor had no other information on him, couldn't even tell me what he was a "doctor" of, and had no idea why Danny might have been interviewing him. I decided to rattle Jekyll's cage and see if he scurried away anywhere interesting.

All of this was running willy-nilly through my head on the way to the Water Department. When I arrived the wind had calmed but it was still overcast. The building's proximity to where Danny's body was found, my memory of him lying in that alley, sharpened my teeth to a fine edge. That was jake with me. I was looking to throw a scare into this Jekyll character, so a foul mood was just what I needed.

Once I found the right office, I bulled my way past his secretary and found Jekyll behind his desk, cleaning his specs.

"What's the meaning of this?" he said as though he was reading right out of the handbook for cliché dialogue.

Right on cue his secretary said, "I tried to stop him, Dr. Jekyll, but he wouldn't listen."

I decided to get his attention right away.

"I'm investigating a murder, Dr. Jekyll. I have a few questions for you."

His eyebrows did a little dance. Not a flamenco, but a quick jig. I could see his mind dancing even faster.

"That's alright, Miss Emery. I'll speak with the gentleman. You can go back to your desk . . . and shut the door."

He stoically finished cleaning his specs and put them on.

"Do I need a lawyer present for these questions?"

"I don't know. Do you?"

"Are you with the police, Mr. . . . ?"

"Slade—Dirk Slade. I'm not a cop, just a private investigator."

I could see the fact I wasn't the real heat was a relief to him.

"Then I think I can forego legal representation," he said smugly.

"What murder are you talking about, Mr. Slade? And how does it concern me?"

"The victim was Danny Legget, a reporter for *The Daily Specter*." He tried not to react to the name, but that alone revealed plenty. "I'm told he recently interviewed you for a story."

He pretended to think about it.

"Legget? I don't recall that name. I've been interviewed many times by reporters, but not recently. What would the story have been about?"

I didn't want him to know I was in the dark about what Danny was working on, so I asked again. "You're certain you weren't contacted by anyone from the *Specter* recently?"

"I'm certain, Mr. Slade."

I decided I'd stirred the pot enough. It was time to let him simmer.

"Alright, Mr. Jekyll. I guess my information was faulty. I appreciate your time."

"It's *Dr.* Jekyll," he said stiffly.

"Oh, sorry. *Dr.* Jekyll." I moved towards the door, then turned back. "Just curious. Are you a medical doctor?"

"I have a Ph.D. in biochemistry. Why do you ask?"

"No reason. I figured it wouldn't be a podiatrist or a gynecologist running the water works."

The next part of my job was the toughest. Waiting. I set up in the Packard where I'd have a good view of anyone coming or going from Jekyll's building, and waited.

It was such a drab gray day I almost fell asleep. Fortunately, Kink showed up—or rather popped in.

"Hey, Bud. On a stakeout?"

"How'd you know where I was?"

"I always know where you're at, Bud," she said, taking a seat on the steering wheel. "I've got your inner frequency on tap. It's a fairy magic thing. Don't ask me to explain it. I don't do science."

"Which is it, science or magic?"

She shrugged and her wings flittered.

"So what's the story, morning glory? Whose tail put you on this trail?"

"Stop with the rhymes already, Kink. You're bringing my hangover back from the dead.

"I'm waiting for the water department guy to leave. I rousted him earlier, and I just want to see where he goes, who he talks to."

"Did he kill Danny?"

"I don't know. I don't even know if he has any connection to the case. But he's the only lead I've got right now."

She took wing and hovered next to the windshield, looking for I-didn't-know-what.

"You need any muscle?"

"No. Thanks anyway, Kink. I think I can handle this guy."

"Alright. Oops, I'm getting a tingle on another frequency. See you later, gator."

"Speaking of gators . . . ." Before I could ask about her friends in the club the night before, she was so much Kink-shaped smoke.

Her timing was good though. When I looked up, I saw Jekyll pull out into the street, driving a Buick Roadmaster. I started up the Packard and followed.

If Jekyll had been rattled by my brazen appearance in his office, he didn't show it. I followed him to the dry cleaners, a bakery, a gas station, and then to, what I assume was, his home. At that point I figured he was a dead end, but I had nowhere else to be, so I sat on him. While I played the waiting game, the sun surrendered its post and darkness swept in to stand guard over the city like a brooding sentry. It wasn't long before the night was as black as a crow's wing.

As far as I could tell, Jekyll lived alone. Through his windows I could see his silhouette moving around, but I didn't see a wife or anyone else. I was starting to wish Kink would make another appearance just to relieve the boredom, when Jekyll came out and started up the Roadmaster. I was in gear before he was. I followed him for several miles—he was the slowest driver I'd ever seen, so the only problem was keeping the Packard far enough back that he wouldn't spot me. He went all the way out to the eastern edge of town.

By the time he reached his destination, a billowing fog had rolled in as if on a cinematic cue. James Whale couldn't have timed it better himself, for it seemed Jekyll's port of call was the local cemetery. I figure at least the fog would make it easier for me to follow him undetected.

It was dead quiet, so I didn't shut the Packard's door all the way. I trailed Jekyll from some 40 feet back, but I could have been closer. He never turned around. He knew right where he was going. He had to have been there before.

He finally stopped in front of a family mausoleum. Right away another figure joined him. This new character was a tall, angular fellow with a pointed chin. He was wearing a trench coat not unlike mine, but I didn't recognize him. It was obvious they knew each other though, and this clandestine meeting told me just what I needed. The good doctor was up to something illegitimate, and the odds were it was connected to Danny's murder.

Very slowly, working my way behind the largest tombstones I could find, I tried to get close enough to hear what they were saying.

There was something, or someone, just behind this new player. It looked like just another memorial statue, but it was hidden in the shadow of the mausoleum, so I couldn't be sure. Whatever it was, it was big and bulky. For a moment I thought I saw it move slightly, but at night, in a graveyard, your mind can play tricks on you.

I was close enough I could tell Jekyll and the other fellow were arguing, though I could only catch a word or two. This other guy held out something. I couldn't tell what it was, but it was small enough to fit in his hand. Jekyll tried to take it, but the fellow pulled it back. They argued some more. I gathered what was going on was akin to blackmail. The stranger had something Jekyll wanted, and he was making demands.

When his argument, whatever that was, fell on deaf ears, Jekyll stomped off towards his car. He obviously wasn't getting what he came for.

I knew where to find Jekyll if I wanted, so I decided to stay with the other fellow. He started off in the opposite direction and I followed. He didn't go far. He stopped and I heard talking. Then the shadow I thought was a statue scuttled off in a totally different direction. Suddenly I heard a noise that sounded like stone grinding against stone, and a resounding *whoosh* of air. I couldn't tell for sure in the fog, but it looked like my statue had flown away.

Having left my wings at home, I stayed on my original target. He was in no hurry as he walked off, so it was easy to track him. At least until he disappeared. I mean he vanished. Fog or no fog, I was right behind him. One second he was there, the next he was gone.

I spent another 20 minutes searching for him. All I found was his coat—at least it might have been his. I gave up and went home.

9

HYDE AND SEEK

The sun surmounted the horizon in glorious fashion, and the day began to eat the night like a snake devouring its own tail. It was a surprise appearance. With all the rain, I hadn't seen a sky full of sunshine in a while. However, the dawn didn't hold any new clues for me. With no new leads on Danny's case, I decided to get back to the job of finding the Prince kid. I called his home first, to make sure he hadn't showed up. Renfield answered and told me, "No, the young master has not returned."

So I got in the Packard and headed for the community pool. I had no idea why the Fiends had chosen the pool as their stomping grounds. I could only guess that because they were primarily a teenage gang, they had some connection to it. Or maybe that's where they figured they could get other kids hooked on their dope. I did know their head honcho. He wasn't a swimmer or a teenager.

Eddie Hyde was a brute of a man. I'd dealt with him many times when I was on the force. He'd been in and out of jail for an assortment of crimes—mostly violent. How he'd come to be in charge of a bunch of overgrown ankle biters, I didn't know.

I know what you're thinking. You're thinking Hyde and the bookish Dr. Jekyll are the same person. They're not—not even close. It's only movie magic that makes you think so. Two different actors—two different people.

When I got to the pool, I didn't see much activity at all. The weather hadn't been conducive to swimming lately, and there were only a couple of kids and some older folks in the water for their morning swim. The Creature from the Black Lagoon was up on his lifeguard stand, sunning himself like an overgrown crested gecko. He looked only half awake.

There was a burger joint right next to the pool, and that's where I saw some of the local hoods gathering. I didn't spot anyone who resembled John Prince, but it wasn't long before I recognized Hyde. He came out of a nearby auto repair shop and claimed the picnic bench next to the burger place. The hoods who'd been sitting there let him have it to himself.

He sat there eating sunflower seeds and spitting the shells at any pigeon brave enough to come within range looking for scraps.

I made my way over. When I got close, a couple of ragged-looking young toughs moved in front of me. One of them pulled a knife and said, "One more step and I'll stick you like a pig, then gut you like a fish."

"Make up your mind," I replied. "Am I pork or the catch of the day?"

He got this perplexed looked on his face, but before he could reach any conclusion, Hyde waved them both aside.

"Let the copper through, boy'th," called out Hyde to his minions.

He still spoke with that bit of a lisp I remembered, but then he wasn't the kind of guy to visit a speech therapist.

I walked up and sat across the table from him. His two bodyguards hovered nearby—not that he'd need them. Underneath that derby of his, he was a hulk. Thick, solid muscle from bicep to quad. I knew I wouldn't want to tussle with him.

"I'm not a cop anymore, Hyde. Just a private investigator. I don't care what you and your boys are up to here."

"What mak'th you think we're up to anything?" he sneered, spitting a couple of sunflower shells in my direction.

"Like I said, I don't care."

"Then what do you want, Thlade?" Out of his small mouth, crowded with teeth, my name was *Thlade*.

"I'm looking for a missing kid. I'm told he might have joined up with the Fiends."

"There are lot'th of kid'th working for me, Thlade!" He certainly wasn't shy about his lisp. In fact, he was the kind of guy who spoke with exclamation points. "I'm a bithy man. I can't keep track of them all!"

"Yeah, I heard you've been busy. Running dope, knocking off your rivals, generally pissing all over town to mark your territory."

"A guy'th gotta make a living."

"I would think a gang war costs more than it's worth."

"Unleth you've got a sponthor," he said, smiling.

"What do you mean, *a sponsor*?"

"Leth juth thay I've been doing thum work for Bauth Wolf, tho you and your cop friend'th don't want to meth with me."

"You think the police are afraid of Talbot?"

"Only the honeth one'th."

I knew as well as he did there were people on the force in the pocket of the Wolfman. But I didn't get Boss Wolf's connection with the Fiends. He didn't need a bunch of kids to do his dirty work.

"Why would Talbot pay you to cause trouble? He's got his own men."

Hyde shrugged.

"I didn't think you'd take orders from anyone, Hyde," I said, trying to goad him. It wasn't hard to do.

"I don't take order'th from no one!" he shouted, standing up and slamming his fist on the table. The wood cracked and the nearby hoods went on alert. More importantly, I could see Hyde had a piece tucked in his belt. A big black .45.

He sat back down, visibly took a breath to calm himself, and said, "But I do take thuggethon'th in the form of cash."

"Suggestions, huh? I'd suggest a trip to the dentist might be in order. Those sunflower seeds can be a periodontal nightmare."

"Keep it up, funny man, and they're gonna be yoothing a magnet to get all the iron out of you."

I decided not to inform him bullets were made of lead and copper, not iron, and that neither were magnetic.

"Like I said, Hyde, I don't care about what you're up to. I'm looking for a John Prince. His father would probably make it worth your while if you would hand him over."

"Don't know anybody by that name."

"Mind if I ask some of your boys?"

"Go ahead. They won't know anybody by that name either."

Which told me I'd get zero cooperation from any of the Fiends.

"Like I said, his father's got dough. He's lousy with it. So it might be worth your while. Here's one of my cards. If you run across him, call me."

I laid one of my business cards in front of him. He looked at me with a gravedigger's stare, picked it up, tore it in two, and spit some more sunflower seed shells at me.

Maybe because the sun was out in force, I decided to look on the bright side. At least they weren't bullets.

10

A FAMILIAR RING

S o far my leads in both cases had taken me nowhere but down a cul-de-sac crowded with belligerent rejects, a reprobate biochemist, and an adobe boy toy. Pretty soon I was going to need a program to catalog all the players. It gave me a pre-hangover headache just thinking about it, but no one else had been elected.

I knew Jekyll was involved in something shady, but I didn't know what. The unknown pair he'd met at the graveyard were suspects, but so were Katia and her golem. I knew Hyde and Boss Wolf were involved in something out of the ordinary, but I didn't know what was behind it. And I didn't know if the Prince kid really had any connection to the Fiends or not. I had squat.

I fed Alley Cat, let her know I wasn't without affection for her—even though I hadn't been around much—and was just about to pour myself a tall stiff one, when Halloran called. They'd found something at a crime scene they thought might be Danny's and wanted me to confirm.

I jumped in the Packard and violated several traffic laws in my rush to get there. *There* turned out to be a loft apartment located directly above the *Gray Gallery*, the local art museum. I was surprised to see a real estate FOR SALE sign on the front door. Slapped over it was single slat reading SOLD.

I made my way upstairs, just in time to see a body being wrapped up by the coroner's assistants. I recognized the dead man, despite the rigid mask the Grim Reaper had carved into his face. He was the same fellow who met Jekyll in the cemetery. The one I'd followed and lost.

"Slade, over here." Halloran waved at me.

"Who's the stiff?" I asked.

"Name's Jack Griffin," said Halloran, reaching into his bag of popcorn for another handful. "In case you don't recognize him, he was the Invisible Man. We've got a long list of crimes he's suspected of having a part in, but we never got the goods on him."

Well that explained how he vanished in the graveyard. But it didn't tell me how he was connected to Danny. Except that I could see this place had been turned inside out just like Danny's.

"What did you find?"

Halloran pulled a ring out of his pocket and handed it to me. "Does this look familiar?"

It was Danny's San Diego State class ring. He'd gone back to school and graduated after the war.

"It's Danny's," I said, handing it back.

"I thought so," said Halloran, pushing his hat even further back on his head than usual. I knew that meant he was thinking overtime—that he was as baffled as I was.

"You find anything else?"

"Nothing that would connect him to Danny. No wallet, no notebook. Griffin lived here with his *boyfriend*." He pointed at the distraught fellow Groves was interviewing across the room. "Apparently the boyfriend came home when the killer was still here."

"You know, I went to Danny's apartment that night you found him. It looked just like this," I said, motioning at the disarray.

"I know. We went there too. It doesn't mean anything. Whoever took Danny's wallet had his address and keys, and decided, with him dead, it would be easy pickings. As far as this place goes, I figure he must have had a partner-in-crime, and they had a falling out. Whoever it was, was looking for Griffin's share of the loot."

"You think it was the boyfriend?"

"I doubt it," said Halloran. "He doesn't look the type. Besides, the coroner says the bruises on Griffin's neck look just like the ones on Danny. Somebody with oversized paws."

I agreed. One look at the boyfriend and I could see he couldn't strangle a mouse. He was young, handsome, but the epitome of the anemic fellow in the old Charles Atlas ads who got sand kicked in his face.

"There is one thing that's very peculiar," said Halloran. "You'll find out eventually, so you might as well know. Danny's death wasn't as cut-and-dried as I suspected. I'm not certain it was just a mugging after all."

"Why do you say that?"

"The coroner says Danny's lungs were full of water. The cause of death was drowning."

I was as stunned as I probably looked. I'd never bought the mugging thing, but drowning?

"There wasn't enough rain in that alley to drown a rat," stated Halloran, "so Danny's body must have been moved after he was killed, and dumped there. Why, I don't know."

There were a lot of reasons for moving a body. The first being you didn't want it found where you lived . . . or worked . . . or anywhere a witness could place you. As for the bruising, it likely meant the owner of those large hands had them wrapped around Danny's neck and held him under until he drowned.

"The swish's name is Dorian Gray," said Groves, leaving the boyfriend weeping on his sofa. "He owns the art gallery downstairs, or did until he sold the building recently. He says he only caught a glimpse of the killer, and that he was big and dark-colored, and left through the window."

"We're three stories high," I said.

"What was your first clue, Sherlock, the stairs?" ragged Groves, obviously peeved I was even there. To Halloran he added, "I checked. There's no fire escape, no building close by. The window he says the guy went out of is a 30-foot drop."

"You think he's lying?" asked Halloran.

"I don't think so," said Neanderthal cop. "He might be seeing things. You know how hysterical they can get."

"Groves," I said with a big sigh, "why is it when you think, I smell meat burning?"

He flashed me a dirty but confused look. I don't think he got the reference.

So, something big and dark apparently flew out the window. That sounded a lot like the shadowy figure I saw with Griffin in the cemetery. The one that appeared to go up, up, and away. And the item Griffin wouldn't turn over to Jekyll had to be Danny's notebook. I had no proof of that, but I was as sure of it as I was that zombies are necrophiliacs.

Since I couldn't be certain, I didn't see any reason to share my suspicions with Halloran and his lap dog. But now I had a real connection between Danny, the Invisible Man and his airborne accomplice . . . and Dr. Jekyll . . . the director of the Water Department.

His lungs were full of water. It didn't require great detective work.

Danny's words hit me again—like a sucker punch.

Start drinking your Scotch straight."

11

A WHISPER OF NYLON

Morning crawled out of the dark like a tortured soul escaping from hell. I crawled out of bed with a hell of a hangover. My legs wobbled, my head throbbed, and as if I wasn't in bad enough shape, Alley Cat crossed my path and almost caused me to fall face first onto the linoleum. I figured all that black fur of hers didn't bode well for my investigation.

Nevertheless, I spent the day driving up and down the streets of Monster Town, checking every place I could think of where a runaway teen might hang out. I might as well have been looking for a splinter in a woodchipper. Nobody knew him, no one had seen him, and not a soul wanted to talk to a nosey old private dick like me.

I finally gave up and headed for the *Sanctuary*. I not only wanted a drink, I wanted to talk with Star again. I was certain she knew more about what Danny was working on than she said, and I was determined to get it out of her. At least that's what I told myself.

I was also hoping to find Kink. I was one for two. Star was nowhere to be seen, but Kink was entertaining a table full of mole people. She'd gotten them laughing so hard they were beginning to stink—which mole people tend to do when subjected to an excess of hilarity.

I got her attention and pulled her away from the table, much to the relief of the other customers.

"Kink, I need you to put out the word with your sources. I'm looking for a kid name of John Prince, and I've hit a wall. He's a runaway."

"Son of Dracula?"

"Yeah, that's him. You've heard something?"

"No," said Kink. "I just know the name. I'll put out the word, but it's a mess out there right now."

"What do you mean?"

"I mean felonies, misdemeanors, general lawlessness and anarchy. It's a war zone."

"What are you talking about, Kink?"

She looked at me like I was some kind of chucklehead. "Some private eye you are," she declared. "You need to get out and open those peepers of yours, or ask your cop friends. They've got more business than they can handle. Between the crime and the arson, it's almost as if someone's trying to give Monster Town a black eye."

I'd heard that before somewhere. It was Neanderthal cop talking about Danny and his stories.

"Alright, Kink. I get it. The streets aren't safe. Just let me know if you hear anything on the Prince kid."

"You got it, Bud."

She buzzed back to her mole friends, and I waited until Quasi had a free moment.

"Where's Star tonight, Quasi? Isn't she singing?"

He shook his head. "She was here earlier, but she wasn't feeling good. She went home."

"Where's home?"

He looked at me with his one good eye and scratched his hump. "I shouldn't tell you that. She may not want company."

"I'm not looking for company, Quasi," I said, not sure if I was lying or not. "I just have to ask her a couple of questions about a case I'm working on."

"Is it about Danny?" he asked.

I nodded and he gave me her address.

It wasn't a very nice place. The outside was rundown, the paint faded and cracking. The elevator didn't work, the stairway door was hanging crooked, and the corridor leading to Star's apartment smelled of mildewed carpet and the dreary anonymity of a multitude of wasted lives.

It surprised me that this was where she lived. Yet, for some reason, I wasn't so surprised when she opened her door and I could tell she'd been crying. It didn't take a skilled shamus to figure it out. Her eyes were puffy, her cheeks damp. She was wearing an old white robe, which she clutched modestly just under her throat.

"Mr. Slade," she said as she wiped her face to no avail. "What are you doing here?"

"I just had a few more questions for you. Can I come in?"

She hesitated.

I could see it in her eyes. Part of her wanted to let me in, and part of her was frightened of the idea. I didn't understand the fear part, but I decided to interpret her silence as a *yes*. I stepped through the door. She didn't try to stop me. Instead she said, "You'll have to excuse me for a minute."

She shut the door behind me and vanished into what I assumed was her bedroom. I took off my hat and used the opportunity to look around.

The interior of her place certainly didn't match the exterior. The decor was nouveau Hollywood, with white faux fur throw rugs, chrome-edged furniture, and decorative Chinese lantern lights. It was like something right out of a Beverly Hills advertisement—a film star's boudoir on-the-cheap. She even had movie magazines scattered about on various lacquered tables.

I knew then Janice Starlin wasn't just a wannabe, she was an *I-will-be*.

When she finally emerged from her bedroom, she didn't simply walk out, she made an entrance. There was no hint of the damp-faced, robe-wearing, doleful woman who had answered the door. She'd put on a cream-colored skirt, nylons, and a lacy white blouse that didn't conceal much. She was in full war paint, and her ebony hair was perfect. How she'd transformed herself so quickly, I had no idea. I guess she'd had a lot of practice.

She caught me staring, but ignored it.

"Would you like to sit?"

I did, on her snow-white sofa. I hoped none of my gumshoe grime would rub off.

"Would you like a drink?" she asked in a voice like melted butter on mashed potatoes.

"Sure. Whatever you've got."

"I've got Scotch. I believe that's your drink."

"Mostly."

It wasn't just her appearance that had changed. She came out of that bedroom with a whole different attitude. I could see it on her face—even in the way she carried herself. And a beautiful carriage it was. I watched her go to her kitchenette, thinking one thing hadn't changed. She was still wearing that body to die for. However, I wasn't ready for a cold slab in the morgue just yet.

She came back with a Scotch-rocks for me and what looked like ginger ale for herself. She sat in the armchair opposite me and crossed her legs.

She'd ordered a virgin margarita the other night, so I was curious.

"You don't drink?"

"Not anymore."

I sipped my Scotch. She absentmindedly stirred her drink with a finger.

"So, what other questions did you have, Mr. Slade?"

"First I wanted to tell you that your tip about Dr. Jekyll paid off."

"How so?"

"I spoke with him. He wasn't very forthcoming, so I followed him. He met up with a guy the police now suspect was Danny's killer. That guy is also now dead."

She tried to disguise it, but I could see that scared her. She pulled out a cigarette from a case on the end table and lit it. I was more certain than ever she knew more about what was going on than she'd told me.

69

I decided to press her.

"Do you know someone named Jack Griffin?"

"No. Was he the man who killed your friend, Danny?"

"It looks like it. But, obviously, he wasn't the only one involved."

"Did you find the notebook?"

"No, it's still missing." I thought it strange she asked about the notebook, but not about Jekyll or who might have killed Danny's killer. "I spoke with Quasimodo at the *Sanctuary*, and he told me you talked at length with Danny at least a couple of times," I lied, playing a hunch. "That's not what you told me. You made it sound as if you'd hardly spoken with him at all."

My hunch was right. I saw it on her face.

"Sure," she said. "I talked with Danny a couple of times."

"Why?"

She took a deep breath like she was making a decision. "Because I was paid to give him something."

"Give him what?"

"It was a large envelope," she said as if the revelation itself were dangerous. "I don't know what was in it."

"You didn't look?"

"No," she replied as if even the suggestion of knowing what was in the envelope terrified her. "But Danny did—right there in front me. It was just a bunch of papers. Whatever was on them, though, excited him."

"Who paid you to give it to Danny?"

She turned her head and looked away. "I can't tell you that."

I saw how frightened she was, so I tabled that question for the moment.

"Danny didn't say anything about the papers when he looked at them?"

"Just what I already told you. He read aloud something about a Water Department report and Jekyll's name. That's all I remember."

"Didn't he wonder where you got the papers?"

She shook her head.

"He never asked who gave you the envelope?"

"No!" She sounded more angry than scared this time. Then, with more control, she said, "I think he already knew."

"So he knew ahead of time that someone was going to pass this information to him."

She shrugged and looked away again.

"Why didn't you just tell me all this when I first asked you?"

"I didn't know you," she said. "You said you were Danny's friend, but you could have been anybody."

That could have been the way it was, but I wasn't buying it.

"What are you afraid of, Star? Why do you look like a filly ready to bolt? What are you trying to run away from?"

She looked at me hard—hard enough to wilt lettuce. She took a drag of her cigarette and exhaled.

"In *Out of the Past*, Jane Greer is running from her shady ex-boyfriend, Kirk Douglas. He's hired a detective to find her," she said as if it were the natural response to my question, and the not the obscure reference it seemed to be. "I loved her in that movie."

Her expression changed, but to what I wasn't sure. It wasn't fear on her face, or anger or doubt. It was more like resignation.

"We're all running away from something," she said as plain as if she were telling me the time of day. "What are you running away from, Mr. Slade?"

It was a lucky punch, but I felt it all the same.

I took a sip of my Scotch and considered what she'd told me. Her story had more holes than her lace blouse, but when she uncrossed her legs to the whisper of nylon, and then crossed them again, I was ready to fill in the gaps myself.

Yeah, I was an idiot—a stark raving nincompoop. I was in the middle of an investigation, trying to find the killer of my best friend, and all I could think of at that particular moment was that I wanted to run my hands up those nylons. I wanted her. I wanted her bad.

I'd even convinced myself that I liked her, felt a little sorry for her. There was a certain charm about her mysteriousness. But she could turn it off as quickly as she turned it on.

She stood and put her drink down.

"I think you'd better go," she said as cold as a frozen fish.

"Alright," I responded, trying to match her chill.

I grabbed my hat, but when I stood my bum leg stiffened. I limped more than usual on my way to the door.

"What's wrong with your leg?" she inquired.

"An old wound. It acts up now and again."

"What happened?"

"A bullet took a dislike to my thigh."

I opened the door and turned to say goodbye. She was right there behind me, only inches away. The look on her face wasn't so chilly anymore. It was vulnerable, imploring. She moved closer—close enough I could feel her body heat. At that proximity she smelled like maple syrup. She put her right hand to my chest and pleaded, "Please don't tell anyone what I told you."

"I won't," I said, beginning to sense a familiar stirring. "But I need to know who gave you the envelope."

"I can't." She turned her head briefly away, then looked up into my eyes once more. "Please don't ask me." She pressed herself even closer.

I put on my fedora, still looking down at her. She wanted to be kissed. I could see that. It was as plain as the quiver on her lips. I didn't know if she was trying to seduce me or just keep me dangling on the line. Whatever she was doing, it was working.

With more will power than I knew I had, I said, "So long."

I turned and walked out.

12

IF LOOKS COULD KILL

y next move was to go see Boss Wolf. Not that I wanted to. I really didn't. It wasn't so much that I was afraid of him, though there was a lot to fear. It had more to do with my aversion to canines. I'd deal with it, because I figured Talbot might be willing to help me find the missing kid, if for no other reason than John Prince was a friend of his own son.

It was the first really warm day in a while. Driving through town, I imagined I saw more smiles than usual. Even the shadows were light and airy. My own mood was unexplainably upbeat as well. That changed once I got to Talbot's place.

There were goons all over—outside and in—and all armed to the overbite. Goblins, ogres, trolls, and a couple ugly enough they could have passed for monsters, even if they weren't. It was such an unsightly group they made me look like Cary Grant. I would have settled for Robert Mitchum.

The first one I ran into made a call on a sort of guardhouse phone in a booth just outside the place, and, after a quick search of my person, let me pass. All the muscle had me wondering again. Why would Boss Wolf be using a penny ante gang like the Fiends? If he wanted something done, all he had to do was snap his shaggy fingers.

Talbot had certainly done alright by himself. He had a sprawling single-story place with a modern design and an expansive swimming pool area decked out as a pseudo tropical lagoon. Laid out next to the pool, sunning herself, was the same chippie Talbot had been with at the *Sanctuary*. She didn't have a stitch on, which was jake with me.

After another search I was admitted to the house itself, and led to a cozy living room, where I was immediately assaulted by an array of odors, not the least of which was wet dog. I was guessing someone had just gotten out of the pool.

"The boss will be with you when he's ready," said my gruff guide, leaving me on my own.

I looked around, but there wasn't much to see. It was a pretty typical looking place. It could have been right off the set of *Leave It To Beaver*. You'd never guess it belonged to the biggest gangster in Monster Town.

I was thinking I might as well sit down, when the dolly by the pool walked in. She was wearing one of those silk kimono robes that go down about mid-thigh. I'd say she was showing off those stems of hers again, except she hadn't bothered to tie the robe very tight. I guess she was showing off her tan.

I doffed my hat out of habit. She glanced at me as if I were a new piece of furniture. She found and opened a velvet cigarette case, took out a smoke, and closed it. There was a fancy lighter right next to the case, but instead of using it she walked straight up to me.

"Got a light?" she asked, barely looking at me.

I lit her up. She didn't thank me, but turned and looked out a window. I guess she thought her half-naked profile was thanks enough.

"Dirk, wasn't it?" she asked, still looking out the window.

"Still is," I replied. "You're June, right? Or do you prefer Leech Woman?"

She smiled and looked straight at me for the first time. "You recognize me?"

The thought that I knew her from the big screen had her beaming. I didn't want to dash her illusions of grandeur by telling her Kink had tipped me off, so I said, "Sure."

"Not many people do," she said, walking away, her voice more maudlin. "I was just a one-hit wonder."

I didn't want to mention the film was hardly a hit, so I decided to commiserate.

"That's more than most people have."

She turned to look at me again, but didn't say anything. It was as if she were studying me . . . or looking over a side of beef hanging in a butcher shop window. She took a puff, blew out a gray-white smoke ring, then probed it suggestively with her finger. She glanced over at me with one of those half-sly, half-seductive looks women use, apparently to see if I'd gotten the message. It would have been more subtle with a megaphone.

"What do you want, Slade?"

At the sound of Talbot's gritty voice, she furtively tightened her robe and turned to greet him.

"I was just asking him the same thing," she said.

Talbot looked at what she was almost wearing and said, "Go get dressed."

She didn't say a thing, but ambled off with a little shake of her behind. Talbot didn't see it. His large, deep-set eyes were focused on me.

He looked much the way I remembered from the old days, when he was still small-time and the cops would lean on him and get nothing. He wasn't tall but he was beefy, all of it muscle—very hairy muscle. His mitts were bigger than mine, and so was his head. The trimmed beard was new, and the familiar network of burst capillaries across his bulbous nose had spread.

I found his attire amusing, but stifled a snicker. He was wearing charcoal suspenders over a white T-shirt and his enormous wooly feet were bare. It didn't help that his little porkpie hat looked ridiculous on top of his huge skull.

The way he regarded me made it easy to swallow my laugh. It was a white-hot glare. And with eyebrows like his, he could really do a frown justice.

"Well, Slade?" he snarled.

"I'm looking for a missing kid."

The frown disappeared and he chuckled, though it came out more like a belch.

75

"That's rich. You looking for a kid. Maybe if you'd been looking for a kid way back when, you'd still be a cop." He was taunting me, but I had nothing for him. "Of course, if you were a cop, you wouldn't be standing there. I don't like cops."

"Except the ones on your payroll."

"Yeah," he laughed and smiled rather acidly, "except those ones."

Up close I could see he wasn't impervious to age. He was starting to get a little heavy around the waist. But who was I to talk? I was getting a whisky belly of my own.

His scowl returned as quickly as it had left. "Why you asking me about some kid?"

"I figured you might help me find him because he's a friend of your son's."

"Harold? You've seen Harold?" His voice softened to almost a hush, and his imposing demeanor did a one-eighty.

"I saw him at school. He was at football practice."

"How is he? How did he look?"

"He looked fine," I said, curious why he was asking me. "He's a fine upstanding lad and a hell of a football player from what I hear," I said, embellishing a tad.

"Good. Good," he said, scratching himself behind his ear in rapid fashion.

He noticed the quizzical look on my face and added, "His mother doesn't really let me see him much. She's as protective as a she-wolf—a real bitch."

"The kid I'm looking for is John Prince. Know him?"

A sliver of surprise shaded his countenance. His throat pulsed a tick.

"Sure, I know the name Prince. Who doesn't? But I didn't know his son was a friend of Harold's."

I could tell by the way he said that there was something he *wasn't* saying. I didn't think it had anything to do with the kid, but the name Prince certainly struck a furry chord. I began to wonder if everyone in this town was keeping secrets, then realized how stupid that sounded even inside my head.

"Well, his father hired me to find him. So, maybe you can think of good reason to put the word out, and let me know if you locate him."

"Okay, alright," he said with unexpected equanimity. Though even as he said it, I could see his mind was working on something else. "I'll put the word out. Couldn't hurt."

"That's all I wanted," I said, replacing my fedora atop my head. "Thanks for your time."

"Sure."

Boss Wolf's thoughts were still elsewhere, so I showed myself out. I didn't know for a fact his absentminded turn had to do with what Hyde told me about the Fiends' association with him, but I was feeling that familiar old gumshoe itch of suspicion that there was a connection. I was sure Talbot's organization was the Fiends' dope connection, but there was something more than that going on. It wasn't why I was there, so I let it blow with the breeze.

I was watched just as carefully exiting as I was entering, but nobody bothered me. I got in the Packard, started it up, and pulled away. As I did, a taxi pulled in behind me. I drove just far enough away not to be obvious and turned to take a look.

Some well-dressed dame got out of the taxi, paid the driver, and stood there as it drove away. I did a double take to be sure. It was Star.

I figured it wasn't a social call, not with Leech Woman on the premises. The only conclusion that made any sense was that Star was working for Talbot. What she was doing for him and why, I had no clue. It didn't make a lot of sense, but it was very possible Talbot was the one who gave Star the envelope she passed to Danny. Why Talbot would want to give a reporter information for a story, I couldn't begin to guess.

I needed to stop guessing and get some answers, so I called Jekyll at the Water Department to tighten the screws. I told him I knew all about his connection with Griffin, the Invisible Man. Even though I wasn't sure what the connection was, I could tell, even over the phone, the bluff had rattled him. He was scared. He told me he'd be working late, and that I should come by his office at six.

The most dangerous animal is one that's backed into a corner. That's where Jekyll was, so I was cautious approaching his office. It was the first time in a long while I wished I was still packing. I was just about to dismiss the thought when I saw the door to Jekyll's office was ajar.

As slowly as I could, I opened the door and scanned the room. There was no one in the outer office. Nothing seemed disturbed. It was as quiet as empty gets. Guardedly, I made my way to the back office where Jekyll's desk was located. That door was all the way open. I paused.

"Dr. Jekyll, it's Slade," I announced, figuring if someone was in there, they'd heard my footsteps by now. There was no reply—no sound at all.

I went in. The room was empty. Jekyll wasn't at his desk. He was on the floor.

I'd never seen a body quite as contorted. I couldn't tell if it was his neck that was broke, or his back—or both. He'd been twisted like a Malibu pretzel. Oddly, his specs were still on his face, though one of the lenses was cracked.

I looked around. There wasn't much on Jekyll's desk for a guy who was working late, but next to his phone was a business card. I picked it up. It had the state seal of California and read, *Neil Foster - Director of Constituent Affairs - Governor's Office*. An address and phone number were printed on the front, and someone had handwritten a local number on the back.

I didn't know if Jekyll was trying to call this Foster, or what business he might have with the director of constituent affairs. I figured it could have been any number of things.

I put the card in my pocket and used a handkerchief to open a few drawers. There was nothing out of the ordinary—nothing with criminal overtones. The drawers were filled with the usual, along with pages of water volume reports, water quality assessment tests, and sheets with column after column of numbers. More to the point, there was no notebook. Not that I really expected to find it. The last I could figure, Jekyll didn't have Danny's notebook—Griffin did. Someone else likely had it now. Jekyll might never have gotten his hands on it.

I didn't have a lot of facts, just a bunch of theories. The bodies were piling up like Lincoln Logs, and I still didn't know how they were connected . . . I just knew they were.

I decided I better haul my caboose out of there. I hated to have Jekyll's secretary find him like this, but I didn't want to have to explain to the cops why I was there. Halloran would know I'd been holding out on him. Not that he expected me to share, but he'd have too many questions—waste too much of my time.

I was about to fade when I spotted a couple of sunflower seed shells on the floor. They could have been left by anyone. I could have tracked them in myself from outside. Or they could have been spit out by the killer. That left me with a few hundred suspects at least. One came to mind rather quickly. I'd seen that Eddie Hyde had a taste for the seeds. But what possible connection would he have had with Jekyll? Of course, Hyde was on Boss Wolf's payroll. That begged the question, why would the Wolfman want Jekyll dead? Was he covering his tracks? Was he connected to Danny's death? It wasn't the strangest thing about this case, but it was on the list. Hyde kills Jekyll? That was too trite to be for real.

13

TROUBLED WATERS

Kink popped in for a visit the next day, smelling of a wild night on the town. I told her she should bottle the aroma and call it *Kink's Night Out*. She said I was no daisy either and added a few choice words of Fairyspeak I wasn't privy to. I changed the subject and told her I was going to pay our old friend Bruce a visit. Naturally she wanted to tag along. Of course that meant she was constantly fiddling with the Packard's radio, looking for a station that was playing some new kind of music she called rock 'n' roll.

"Oh, I forgot," said Kink. "I heard something about your missing kid."

"What?"

"He's definitely joined the Fiends."

"You have any idea where he is?"

She shrugged. "That's all I know. Maybe Bruce has heard something about him."

I doubted it. There'd be no reason for him to know about the kid, and that wasn't why I was bothering him. Not that he would mind. Very little bothered him these days.

Bruce Barton was born with a bit of a physical anomaly. Okay, that might be understating it. He had only one eye—one somewhat outsized eye. Where his right eye should have been were pale folds of skin. His scabrous right ear was deformed and part of his upper lip on the same side was missing. Needless to say, he'd had a hard time growing up. But he'd parlayed his malformed visage into a shot on the big screen. Of course, after he made *The Cyclops*, there wasn't a lot of work for him.

Now he ran a school for blind kids. Sure, laugh all you want, but he was a good guy.

I don't know if working with the blind made him feel like a king, or if he just liked the idea they couldn't see his disfigurement. Either way, he was great with them. You could tell how much they loved him, and he them. It was more than just a job to him, it was his passion.

Before the school got going, when he was doing what he could on the streets to survive, he'd gotten pinched on a minor rap. I'd sprung him and he became an informant for me. I knew he still kept his good ear to the ground, so I wanted to see if he could connect any of the haphazard dots I'd collected.

"Kink, you little scamp," said Bruce when he saw her. "What kind of hell have you been raising?"

"Every kind," said Kink, flitting over to give him a big kiss on his good cheek.

"Good to see you too, Dirk," he said grabbing my hand enthusiastically.

"Always a pleasure, Bruce. How's the school going?"

Bruce didn't have even one eyebrow, but I could still make out the frown on his face.

"Someone just bought our building and sent me papers saying when the lease is up we'll have to move out."

"Kicking blind kids to the street? That's cold," said Kink.

"I'm really sorry to hear that, Bruce. You're doing such good work here."

"I'm not certain where we're going to go yet," he replied. "We had a pretty sweet deal here, and I'm not sure what I can afford."

"Look, I know some people," I said. "I can't make any promises, but I'll see what I can do to help."

"That would be great, Dirk."

"Me too," blurted out Kink. "I'll help."

"Thanks, Kink." He looked wistfully through the glass wall of his office to a room full of kids working with clay. "Now, as much as I'd like to think you two dropped by for a social visit, I've still got one good eye. It tells me you've got questions."

"Did you hear about Danny?" I asked.

He nodded.

"We're trying to track down his killer," added Kink.

I wasn't sure where she got the *we*, but I let it ride.

"Do you have any idea why the Fiends would be working for Boss Wolf?" I asked. "Have you heard anything?"

"I haven't heard a word about that," said Bruce. "But I can tell you one thing. Someone's going out of their way to kick up a fuss. It's not business as usual. No one's being particularly discreet about their criminal activity. In fact, it's as if they want it to be front page news."

Which explained why someone might be passing information to the city's top crime reporter, but not what was behind it all.

"Do you think it has anything to do with this new drug making the rounds?"

Bruce shook his head. "That's just part of it. Sure, this heeb seemed to come out of nowhere recently, but it's not the only illicit commotion. It's as if someone were trying to . . . ."

"Give Monster Town a public black eye?"

"I was going to say damage the town's reputation, but I don't know that it was all that respectable to begin with."

"It doesn't make much sense, does it?" I asked, not expecting an answer.

"I guess you'd have to ask yourself, what's the result? What does giving Monster Town a bad name—a worse name—actually do? I mean, outside of just the public relations part."

"I don't know," I said. "Lower property values?"

He tilted his head and aimed his one eye at me, saying, "Maybe. But who does that benefit?"

I didn't know. It didn't make any more sense than the rest of the case. It just seemed another turn on a very serpentine road.

That evening, around seven, I got a call. It was Star. She had something for me. I didn't bother asking what it was over the phone.

I had plenty of questions for her, and I wanted to see her face when she answered them. And not just because it was such a nice face. I wanted the truth about where she stood in all this. I was determined I wasn't going to be played, not even by a face that could launch a thousand ships.

There were no tears this time when she opened her door, no dowdy robe. She was dressed to distraction in a provocative, satin, pearl-gray number. Her dusky hair was pinned up in the back with an expensive-looking black and silver comb designed like a swarm of wasps. I wasn't sure if she was ready for a night on the town, or a night in. But the getup reminded me once again that her peaks and valleys called for more than just casual exploration.

"Thanks for coming," she said, standing aside so I could step in.

I brushed by her and caught that same scent again. This time there was a hint of vanilla mixed with the maple syrup.

"Sit down," she said. "I'll make you a drink."

I sat, but I didn't wait. "You said you had something for me. I'm hoping it's more than a drink."

She ignored the remark, finished making my drink, and brought it to me. Then she went over and pulled something out of an end table drawer. She handed it to me.

"Danny's notebook?" I looked at her for confirmation, but the truth was I didn't need it. I recognized the ratty old thing right away. It was Danny's alright.

"Where'd you get this?"

"I can't tell you that," she said, sitting across from me. "I'm just a delivery girl."

"Does this delivery come from the same party as the envelope you passed to Danny before?"

She didn't respond, but her eyes affirmed the obvious. I opened it, thumbed through it quickly. Danny's scribbling would take some time to decipher.

"It's not for me to say," she said, then hesitated. "But since it was

Danny's, I think you should give it to his editor."

"Was it Boss Wolf who told you to make that suggestion?"

"I don't know what you're talking about."

She was lying. When she looked up and to the right as if casually checking the time, I knew it. There was no clock on the wall.

"I'm talking about how you're working for the Wolfman. I saw you at his place. So unless he invited you over for high tea, don't bother denying it."

"Okay, I won't." She got up, went to her kitchenette, and made herself a real drink—vodka, it looked like. Apparently she was off the wagon . . . at least for tonight. She lit a cigarette and returned to her seat with the drink.

"Why give it to me?" I wondered out loud. "Why not just take it straight to the *Specter*?"

She shrugged. "I just do what I'm told."

I actually believed she didn't know much more about what was going on than I did. Of course that was what I wanted to believe.

When Danny's notebook went missing, I naturally assumed someone was trying to kill a story he was working on. Now someone wanted, what I assumed was, the same story slapped onto their morning paper. It didn't make any sense.

"There's one thing I want to know before I leave," I said. "Why? Why are you working for Talbot?"

She took a drink, then a drag, exhaled, and snuffed out the butt in a brass ashtray engraved with its place of origin—*Hollywood*. She stood and took a couple of steps, looking away from me.

I waited. A good P.I. learns there's a time to push and prod, and a time to let someone stew in their own silence.

"A long time ago," she started, "when I was very young, when I was drinking a lot—long before I got my big break with *Wasp Woman*—I made some other . . . films. I think you can guess what kind of films they were."

I *could* guess.

"I was desperate, dumb, looking for a quick way to break into the business. I was so drunk most of the time, it didn't even bother me much that most of my co-*stars*—if you can call them that—were monsters."

She turned to look at me. There were tears in her eyes.

I guess she expected to see a raw display of disgust on my face. She was mistaken. If I allowed anything to show, it was compassion. I got up and went to her. She tried to turn away and wipe her tears, but I grabbed her arms and made her look at me.

"I'm guessing Talbot has these films."

She nodded. "He was one of the monsters."

I had a brief mental image of her and the Wolfman in one of those scenes, then quickly erased it.

"So what. So he has some raunchy old films. What can he do with them? How's it going to hurt you?"

"If they were ever made public, my career would be over," she declared, the tears flowing again. "I'd never get another job."

I started to tell her Quasi couldn't care less about her past, then I remembered it wasn't her part-time gig singing at the *Sanctuary* she cared about. That wasn't her "career." That was just a side job. She still had visions of Tinseltown dancing in her head—delusions of becoming a silver screen siren to millions. She wanted it all, and apparently would do anything to get it.

Probably, deep in her heart, she knew as well as I did that fame and fortune were unlikely to ever be her traveling companions. Yet she couldn't give it up. I almost said something. But who was I to tread on the fractured cobblestones of her dreams?

So I didn't say anything. I just looked into her eyes. Somewhere along the way, I got lost. Before I even knew it was happening, we were locked in an embrace, and I was kissing those luscious lips.

Deep in the fanciful labyrinth that was my mind, that foreboding alto sax was playing again. Only this time the harmonic timbre of mystery and danger was imbued with ominous passion.

Two hours later she was asleep and I was sapped. Apparently it had been a long time between bouts for both of us. Either that or she was a better actress than I gave her credit for.

I'd half expected her to turn into Wasp Woman at some point. I didn't know if she could, if she still might, or if it was all Hollywood makeup and special effects. I can't say the element of danger didn't add to the intensity of it all.

As tired as I was, I couldn't sleep. So I retrieved Danny's book and tried to make sense of his most recent notes. It wasn't like reading one of his stories in the *Specter*. It was all piecemeal—stuff he collected from various sources. How he'd make heads or tails of it and turn it into something comprehensible, I had no idea. I guess that's why he was the writer and my oversized noggin was barely good enough for a gumshoe.

It took some time, but bit by bit I got the gist of it. I soon understood Danny's cryptic parting line to me—*Start drinking your Scotch straight*. There was something in the water, something toxic. I was no chemist, so the scribbles about the level of trihalomethanes in the water didn't mean anything to me. Another note about how chemical pollution in the system was causing the old lead pipes to corrode made sense. I didn't know if it was the chemicals or the lead or both that were dangerous, but it didn't take a genius to realize the people of Monster Town were being poisoned—slowly, yet as surely as the coming of sunset in a vampire flick.

There was another notation I couldn't quite read. It said something about the governor's office, but I couldn't decode all of Danny's squiggles. There was one thing that was clear—a name. A familiar name—Neil Foster. The same guy whose business card was on the desk of the late director of Monster Town's Water Department.

My first thought was to wonder why, if he knew about the problem, the governor hadn't made it public—hadn't warned people and done something about it. My second thought was more realistic. The governor was up for reelection in less than a month.

If Danny could prove the governor and his people knew about the water, it wouldn't just lose him an election, it would end his political career. And it would have made Danny's. It would have been the biggest story to ever pass through his typewriter.

I had no doubts now. Danny *was* killed to prevent the story from getting out. Jekyll knew about it, and was working with Griffin, the Invisible Man, and his shadowy partner. They killed Danny and took his notebook. It was also very likely the governor's man, Foster, knew about the water, and was conspiring with Jekyll to keep it quiet.

I had no proof of any of it, except a clandestine meeting in a graveyard and police suspicion that Griffin killed Danny. I could only hope that when I handed over the notebook to Igor, he'd be able to make enough sense of Danny's notes to find the proof and publish it.

The piece of the puzzle I still didn't understand was how Boss Wolf fit into all this? I could understand why he'd want to blow the whistle on the city's bad water, but why all the cloak and dagger with Star? Why not just howl it from the rooftops? Maybe because of who he was, he didn't think anyone would take him seriously. That would make sense. However, it wouldn't explain why he didn't just hand the notebook over to Igor at the *Specter*. Why give it to me?

"Did you figure it out?"

I'd been so wrapped up in my deductive reasoning, I'd forgotten I wasn't in my own bed and that Star was lying next to me, naked. Not an easy thing to forget.

"I think so," I responded.

"What's it all about?"

"From what I was able to cobble together, Danny was working on a story about how the water coming into Monster Town has been poisoned."

"What?" Her reaction told me she really didn't know anything about it. She was as alarmed as anyone naturally would be. She sat up, not bothering to cover herself like most women do. I decided I liked that about her. I'm mean, if you've got it . . . and she had all of it.

"Was it done on purpose?" she asked.

"I don't think so. At least there's nothing in Danny's notes about that. But it's very likely government officials knew about the water and didn't do anything about it. Maybe right up to the governor's office."

"That's horrible," she said. "What's it going to do to people? Are we going to . . . ?" She didn't finish the question, but I knew what she was asking.

"I don't know. I don't know how bad it is or how it's going to affect people. I just know we've got get the word out—let everyone know."

"It's terrible anyone would do that. It's monstrous," she declared. A chill seemed to run through her. She looked up at me with eyes that could have seduced a monk and said, "Hold me."

She didn't have to ask twice. I wrapped both arms around her and gently pulled her to me. Her supple flesh pressed against me was all I needed to be revived. I kissed her good, and in no time we were dancing in the sheets.

When I finally came up for air, I wasn't just sapped, I was spent. I also had a good idea how I wanted to leave this world, and what I wanted to be doing when the curtains came down for the final time. And it had nothing to do with a bullet or a hospital bed.

We lay there for a time before she said, out of the blue, "Where's your gun?"

"I don't carry a gun anymore."

"I thought all private dicks carried guns."

"Not this one. Why do you ask?"

"You know they're going to try and kill you."

"Who?"

She smacked me on the chest. "Who do you think, dummy? The people trying to cover this up. They must have killed Danny. Even if they don't know you have the notebook, they know you've been investigating. They'll come after you."

"I guess that means you really care," I said, poking fun at her concern.

She smacked me again. "Of course I care, you lout."

"Don't worry, I'll watch my backside."

She laid back and stared at the ceiling. I laid there and stared at her.

I'm sure it was just my suspicious nature, but I began to ponder why a gorgeous dame like her would even give a big dumb clod like me the time of day. I vetted several wild scenarios—none of which made any sense—then just decided to accept her at face value. Maybe I had some redeeming qualities I wasn't aware of. Well, I was aware of one.

I lay there until the silence was as loud as a scream, and I couldn't take it anymore. She was still staring off into space, her dusky hair in disarray.

"Are you okay?" I asked.

"Yes. Just daydreaming."

"That can be dangerous."

"You think so?" She turned to look at me. "I think dreams are where we reinvent ourselves."

"What if I like you the way you are?"

She laughed at that, as if it couldn't possibly be true and I'd just said it to be nice. I hadn't.

"You reinvented yourself," she said, smiling. "You used to be a policeman, and now you're a dashing private detective."

"It wasn't because of a dream."

"No? Why *did* you leave the police force?"

I kept quiet until she nudged me.

"I don't really want to talk about it," I said as plain as I could.

She turned on her side and looked at me.

"I told you about my . . . my past. It wasn't a pretty picture, but I painted it for you. I bared my soul to you even before I bared my body. Surely it can't be as bad as that."

"It's worse."

"Tell me." I wasn't sure if the sound in her voice was insistence or pleading—pleading with me to prove she wasn't just another piece of tail I'd forget in the morning.

Truthfully, I don't think it was the tone of her voice, or even what she said. Maybe I decided I'd bottled it up long enough. Maybe I needed to say it out loud to someone.

I decided to spill my guts.

"It was a dark night—moonless I mean. Not that that was an excuse. I'm just telling you like it was. Me and my partner were chasing this crumb bum who'd beaten a call girl practically to death. We had him cornered when he pulls out a gat and starts shooting. We pulled our pieces and fired back. He runs, turns down this dim alley, stopping every few steps to turn and fire at us. We're chasing him, firing back. I'm in the lead and I take a slug to my leg. But I don't go down. I shoot back. Only some kid decides at that moment to poke his head out the back door of his father's restaurant and see what all the commotion is. My shot hits the kid. Kills him."

I got it all out as quickly as I could, but it didn't matter. My gut still felt like someone had buried a sword in it. I turned on my side, away from Star. She moved closer and put her arm around me.

"Your leg, is that why you . . . ?"

"Yeah. It's the limp that won't let me forget."

"It wasn't your fault. You know that."

"Then whose fault was it?"

"Did you get kicked off the police force?" she asked, holding me tighter.

"No. There were no charges. I quit."

"There were no charges because it was an accident."

"That's what everybody said."

"It's true," she insisted.

"What's true is that I killed a 12-year-old boy, and nothing can ever change that."

"What if you help save thousands of people from this poisoned water? Won't that mean something?"

"It'll mean something," I replied. "It just won't change anything."

14

A SHADOW IN THE DARK

This is the part of the movie where the true blue shamus simplemindedly decides to hold on to the damning evidence just a little longer so he can tie up all the loose ends himself, and the big bad guys come and take it from him. I figured I was a little smarter than that.

The first thing I did the next day was take Danny's notebook to Igor at *The Daily Specter*. He was already excited about something else—busy on the phone. He'd just gotten the report from the police on the murder of Dr. Jekyll.

I showed him the notebook, told him what I gathered from what I'd been able to read, and his eyes got so big he looked like he was back in that famous "It's alive!" scene where Frankenstein's monster first begins to move. I also told him what I'd seen myself, and what I'd deduced from it all. He agreed it was potentially the biggest story to ever come across his desk. Of course he'd have to confirm anything he read in the notebook. That, he said, would take time. I told him he'd better not take too long, because people were drinking poison, showering in it, swimming in it—he got the message. I also advised him to lock up the notebook when he wasn't reading it. He agreed and said he had just the safe for the job.

That taken care of, I decided I needed to speak with one Neil Foster, director of constituent affairs for the governor of California. I pulled out his business card and tried the handwritten local number first. It was the Oakley Court Hotel. The nicest one in Monster Town. I asked for him by name, and my call was transferred to his room. He answered.

"Neil Foster?"

"Yes, who's calling?"

"Neil Foster of the governor's office?"

"Yes."

"My name is Dirk Slade. I'm a private investigator. I need to speak with you."

"I'm sorry, Mr. Slade. I'm afraid I don't have the time today. I'm preparing to return to Sacramento."

"You're going to want to delay that trip, Mr. Foster."

"Why's that? What's this all about?"

"It's about a trio of murders, including that of Dr. Henry Jekyll. I believe you're acquainted."

When he didn't answer right away, I knew I had him.

"It's also about some water quality reports he had in his desk."

"When do you want to meet?" was all he said.

"How about in an hour at *Maddie's Place.* It's a little cafe—"

"I know it," he said abruptly. *"I'll see you in an hour."*

He hung up without so much as a goodbye. That was jake with me. I could almost taste the butter pecan.

I made sure Alley Cat had some food and a little one-on-one attention, then walked to *Maddie's Place.* I grabbed a booth in the back where we could talk at least semi-privately. I wanted to meet him in public, just in case, but not where he'd be afraid to open up. I wasn't sure what I was hoping he would admit to me, but I had to feel him out. I'd know the truth once I saw his eyes, no matter what kind of prevaricated bureaucratic crap spewed off his tongue.

I started to order the usual—black coffee and butter pecan ice cream—then decided it was a good time to cut back on the joe, seeing as how it was made with the local water. It wasn't exactly a nutritious lunch, but the only thing I liked better than plain butter pecan was a buxom blonde lathered with the stuff. Which made me think. She wasn't blonde, but I wondered how Star's maple syrup flavor would go with butter pecan.

I was only halfway through my mid-day treat when he walked

in—right on time. He had big ears, small beady eyes, and the long delicate fingers of a pickpocket. Judging by the suit he was wearing, he was strictly from Dixie. The creases of his pants were sharp enough to slice bread. Yet, as corny as he was dressed, there was something slick about him. I didn't know if it was in his face or the way he walked. Maybe slick wasn't the right word. Maybe slimy was a better one. Or maybe I was just prejudiced by my expectations.

He walked right up to me. Either he was a good guesser or he'd done some homework.

"Mr. Slade, I presume."

"You presume correctly. Have a seat."

He did and I started to call Maddie over to see what he'd have.

"Nothing for me, thank you." As he said it I could see he was hesitant to even touch the table between us. Apparently *Maddie's* wasn't up to his standards.

"What's this about murders, Mr. Slade? And what does it have to do with me?"

"To be honest, Mr. Foster, I'm not certain what your connection with the murders is, though I have my suspicions. But I know you were in contact with Dr. Jekyll, and that he was in possession of information that the water being pumped into Monster Town is toxic."

I expected him to deny any knowledge of the reports. He took another tack.

"Those were preliminary reports that showed mild levels of lead in the water. Subsequent tests proved the water was fine," he said placidly, as though the issue were nothing of significance. He was very convincing. "I understand they get those blips in the tests all the time. That's why they're always retesting it."

"I see. Then you'd have no objection to my turning over Danny Legget's notebook to *The Daily Specter* so they can confirm or deny reports of problems with the water."

"Legget?" He said it like he was trying to place the name, but I saw the lie in the furrow of his brow.

"Danny Legget," I repeated. "A reporter for the *Specter*." I was getting fed up with people denying they knew Danny's name.

"Oh yes, the reporter. I believe Dr. Jekyll mentioned him. Said he was on some kind of crusade, but that he'd gotten his facts all wrong."

"That doesn't sound like Danny."

He put on a smile—the kind of well-practiced plastic grin people wear when they have something condescending to say.

"I'm sure, Mr. Slade, as a former police officer, you know how reporters can often get carried away when they think they have a story that transcends the mundane copy they write day after day."

So he *had* looked into me.

"I'm not saying Mr. Legget would have rushed into print with anything fraudulent or libelous. I'm certain, given time, he would have found that additional tests proved the water is completely safe."

"Except he didn't have the time. He was murdered."

"Yes, that's right. I remember reading about the death of a reporter in the *Specter*. I hadn't really put the two together. Seems he was the victim of a mugging. Very unfortunate."

He had the expression of a man used to being believed. He was so smug I wanted to smack him. Instead I kept digging.

"So what brings you to our fair city, so far from Sacramento, Mr. Foster?"

"As the governor's constituent liaison, I travel all over the state, listening to the concerns of citizens, handling problems, using the resources of the governor's office to deal with them when I can."

"Problems like potentially bad press?"

"Sometimes," he admitted. "With the election only weeks away, the governor is naturally solicitous to impending issues with public relations. I often troubleshoot those issues. Speaking of which." He pulled a checkbook out of his breast pocket. "In order to prevent any misconceptions among the populace, to forestall any potential bad press as you put it, and prevent any unnecessary panic, I'd like to purchase Mr. Legget's notebook from you. Just to be sure nothing erroneous is published that might have a deleterious effect on the election before it can be recanted. I can assure you the governor would be most grateful."

"How would you explain the payment?" I asked, playing along for the moment. "Checks leave trails."

He shrugged as if it was nothing. "You're a private investigator. We hired you. I assume your dealings with clients are confidential. Even if pressed, we'll say the governor's office hired you to investigate the distressing murder of a respected newspaper reporter. Naturally you'd turn over all evidence of the investigation to us."

When I didn't immediately jump at his offer, he added, "If the idea of a check from the governor's office bothers you, Mr. Slade, I can secure cash."

"What bothers me, *Mr.* Foster, is that people like you would put the results of an election over the health and safety of tens of thousands. Don't get me wrong. I'm not shocked—not even a little surprised. I'm a big boy. I know how the world works. It wouldn't even surprise me to know that you and the governor and assorted other *public servants* have known about the water for some time. It was just never politically expedient to do anything about it."

"Come, come, Mr. Slade. You're imagining conspiracies where there are none."

"Then why are you so interested in getting your hands on Danny's notebook?"

His face went ashen. At that point, I think he realized I wasn't going to cooperate. His façade of diplomacy vanished, replaced by barely restrained anger. I had to give him credit though. He made one last attempt, even if it wasn't a very subtle one.

"All this fuss over a little lead in the water?" He shook his head as if he just couldn't understand it. "We've been using lead pipes all over the state for decades, Mr. Slade. It's practically harmless. And after all, they're already monsters."

That frosted me good, but I restrained myself from choking him out right there in the booth. Maddie didn't need the mess.

"Use those prodigious ears of yours and listen good." I could see I'd hit a sore spot with the ears crack. "I'm not going to give you the notebook . . . or sell it to you. The people have a right to know, and they're going to, whether it costs your boss an election or not. You're just a scab, Foster, covering up an infection that needs to see the light of day. You're nothing but a shadow in the dark."

The gloves were off now. I could almost see the steam rolling out of his substantial ears.

"This won't be the end of it," he said, not bothering to disguise the threat with a smile.

"I'm sure it won't." I got up and stepped out of the booth. Then I leaned down, rested my hands on the table, and got right into his face. His infuriated expression pivoted quickly to one of alarm. He tried to edge away from me, but there was nowhere for him to go. "You know, Foster, I've always wondered what monsters see in *their* nightmares. Now I know."

I walked away, doing my best not to limp. I wouldn't give him the satisfaction.

"Maddie," I called out, loud enough for everyone to hear, "give my friend back there a tall glass of water."

15

CORPORATE CLAWS

When I saw Star that night, I told her about Neil Foster and the restraint I'd shown in not braining him on the spot. She was sympathetic, incredulous that the governor might be involved in a cover-up, and did her best to soothe my savage yearnings. I was frustrated, angry, and really wanted to lay into someone fists first. Star knew it and let me vent awhile before she took matters into her own hands. That's where I was putty . . . at least I was after an hour of her expert soothing.

We didn't talk about much else. She was telling me about an audition she had scheduled for the next day when I passed out. I guess I was even older than I felt. When I woke the next morning, she was already gone.

Even though my night with Star had cooled me down, I was still considering helping Foster take the big sleep myself. I mulled over the possibility calmly, with composure, and decided killing Foster would only leave me at another dead end. Danny was drowned—held underwater by someone who could have overpowered him. Someone with very large hands. There was no way Foster, Jekyll, or even Griffin could have done that to Danny. He may have looked like an easy target, but I knew he was tougher than that. I'd seen him in combat.

There was still at least one someone out there who had a part in Danny's death—the actual killer. For all I knew, there were others involved. I wanted them all. I knew that meant I may not get the hands-on payback I had a yen for, but if I could find some proof against Foster, he was the kind to squeal like a stuck pig and give up his co-conspirators. Finding that proof, however, wasn't going to be easy.

Even though I knew what had happened to Danny, and why, I still couldn't figure how Boss Wolf and the crime spree he was apparently behind was connected. He was obviously at odds with Foster and Jekyll, or he wouldn't have sold them out to Danny in the first place.

I recalled what Bruce and I had discussed about the bad publicity of a crime spree, and the question he'd posed about who benefits from lower property values. The only answer to that was land speculators. But Monster Town wasn't prime real estate to begin with, so excess criminal activity and a front-page story about poisonous water was only going to make local property as attractive as a troll with raging acne. Yet that's what Boss Wolf wanted—apparently.

I had to find out why, and whether it was connected to Danny's death. So I spent a good part of the day at the county recorder's office, researching land deals. Halfway through a ponderous stack of musty documents, I was getting nowhere. Then I remembered something. Actually, I remembered several things that my jumbo-sized thick skull suddenly decided to stitch together. Maddie had told me someone wanted to buy her place, and someone did recently buy both the *Sanctuary* and Bruce's school building. I wouldn't have given it a second thought before, but it occurred to me I'd seen more than the normal amount of real estate signs around town. Many of them already declared they were SOLD. The realization jammed my research into a totally different gear. I looked up each of the transactions I knew about and hit pay dirt.

Bruce's school, the *Sanctuary*, the *Gray Gallery*, and several other recent acquisitions were all purchased by the same company. For some reason, Black Castle Attractions, Inc. was buying up everything in Monster Town it could get its corporate claws on.

I was halfway home when the cops pulled me over. Apparently my old partner had some questions for me. Out of courtesy for a former flatfoot, they let me drive the Packard to the station . . . though they followed close behind and escorted me up to Halloran's desk.

He was behind it, his gray trilby tilted back on his head like he was getting a tan from the fluorescent glow of the station house lights. As usual, there was a bag of popcorn in his hand and crumbs on the vest of his three-piece suit. Neanderthal cop was standing there, handing him a file. I casually sat down.

"Nice of you to drop by, Slade," said Halloran, closing the file.

"I didn't know I had a choice."

"You didn't," snarled Groves.

I ignored him and said to Halloran, "Your mutt seems a tad irritable. Have you checked him for fleas?"

Even Halloran had to chuckle. Groves kind of growled, not knowing he was making my point.

My old partner got serious then. He leaned across his desk and said, "I understand you paid Dr. Henry Jekyll a visit a few days before he was killed. Is that right?"

"That's right."

"His secretary says you bullied your way into his office, pretending to be a police officer investigating a murder. She thinks you killed him."

"She got it wrong," I said, lighting a smoke. "Jekyll sent her out of the room and had her shut the door, so she didn't hear all of it. I told him I was a private investigator."

"Why'd you go see him?"

"I got a lead that Danny had interviewed him recently. I just wanted to see what Danny's interest was, in case it had anything to do with his murder."

"And . . . ?"

"And nothing. It was a dead end. He said my information was wrong, and that he had no recollection of ever speaking with Danny. I thanked him for his time and left."

"I think you came back and tried to beat what you wanted out of him," accused Groves.

I knew I shouldn't, but it was so much fun. I said, "Don't try to think, Groves, you'll pull a muscle."

He came at me and I stood up. His face was in mine and his breath almost knocked me down for the count. I was about to boost him back where he came from, but Halloran horse-collared him and pulled him out of harm's way. That was jake with me. I didn't fancy spending the night in the pokey. The beds in there were as lumpy as week-old oatmeal.

"You know anything about who might have killed Jekyll?" asked Halloran, back in his chair.

"No," I replied, sitting back down. "You have any leads?"

"I've got zilch," he said.

"Look, Slade, I know it won't do any good to tell you to keep your bent nose out of our investigations, but it wouldn't hurt for you to share what you know. Cause I know you've been digging. You must have found out something."

"You first. You have anything more on Danny's murder?"

"Nothing more than I've already told you."

A derogatory noise escaped my lips and Neanderthal cop lost it again.

"We're going to catch whoever killed your reporter friend." he declared, "And we're going find out who knocked off Jekyll."

"Groves, you couldn't find water in a lake."

Groves gritted his teeth and Halloran pressed on.

"What do you know that you're not telling us, Slade?"

I figured I'd throw him a bone, just to get him off my back.

"I don't have any proof, but you might want to look at a fellow named Eddie Hyde for Jekyll's murder."

"The guy who's running the Fiends?" Halloran looked surprised.

"That's the one."

"You want to tell us why we should look at him?"

"No," I said flatly, shaking my head. "But I'll tell you one other thing—just don't ask me how I know. Griffin was working with Jekyll."

"Bull crap!" roared Groves.

"Are you saying Jekyll was involved in Danny's murder?" Halloran seemed skeptical.

"I don't have any hard evidence, but I know they were seen together, along with a third, as yet unidentified, person."

"Before they ended up in the morgue together, I assume," said Halloran.

"That's all I know," I fibbed. "It should give you something to work with though. Can I get out of here now?"

"Sure," said Halloran, scratching his head and looking more confused than ever. "Take a powder."

"Don't let the door hit you in the ass," added Groves.

I got up, put out my butt in Halloran's ashtray, and started to go.

"I do have one more clue for you," I said, getting their attention. "Don't drink the water."

I walked away, enjoying the perplexed looks on their kissers

Before I left the station, I used one of their phones to put in a call to Igor at the *Specter*. I wanted to see what, if anything, he knew about Black Castle Attractions or the land grab that was going on in Monster Town. He was out, so I had to leave a message.

Outside I lit another smoke and stood there for a moment. The night had already consumed the sun, but twilight hadn't yet surrendered to murky darkness. One by one, neon signs sprang to life up and down the boulevard, while the hint of another storm, a massive thundercloud in battleship gray, blew in from the west.

The ride home was uneventful, though I had to pull a quick maneuver after I got lost in thought. This crazy case was getting to me. I decided I'd better concentrate on my driving, get home, have a few belts, and start thinking again tomorrow. Unfortunately, my night wasn't going to go that smoothly.

I was still a dozen feet from my front door when I heard the racket. Someone was inside my place, and by the sound they were tearing it apart. My door was busted—which made me wonder if my neighbors had heard the noise and called the cops. I doubted it. It was that kind of neighborhood.

It didn't matter. I wasn't waiting. I went in. The broken door creaked when I pushed it open. The noise inside stopped.

The lights were out, and only a meager wash of dim light made its way into the room through the window. I thought about making my way to the nearest lamp, but even in the fractured gloom I could see it wasn't there. No doubt it was among the clutter strewn across the floor.

I crouched down and scanned the room. I recognized vague but familiar silhouettes. Then I saw something not so familiar—a shape, a thing darker than the night.

It rushed me. I came out of my crouch to meet it head on and regretted it immediately. I felt like I'd tried to tackle a boulder. I went down with the smell of wet cement in my nostrils. The thing began to pummel me. Its fists were harder than a whore's heart.

"Where is it?" it bellowed with a voice that seemed to echo as it continued to pound me. "Where is it?"

I couldn't defend myself. It knocked my hands away like I was a rag doll. The blows were smothering. I couldn't even come up for air long enough to tell my dense assailant it might want to tell me what *it* was.

"Where is it?"

The pounding stopped. I don't know if it tired or just finally decided to give me a chance to respond. At that point my vision was a little blurry, but my eyes had adjusted enough to the darkness to see what my attacker looked liked. It looked like a gargoyle—a bulky, colorless creature hewn from stone. A pair of stubby horns sprouted from its gritty head, and two massive wings hovered over its back.

The wings were what made it all click for me. This was the thing I'd seen in the cemetery with the Invisible Man. The same thing that had probably killed him, as well as Danny.

"Where's the notebook?" it said with a raspy rumble, its breath like ancient smog. "Where is it?"

"I don't have it," I managed to whisper through bloody lips.

It hit me again . . . and again. I was fading fast. With only a shred of consciousness left, I saw something I was sure must be a pain-induced hallucination. Alley Cat jumped out from wherever she'd been hiding, and hissed liked a crazed cobra. Her hair bristled porcupine-like, and her back was arched in a way that challenged, *Come and get it if you want it.*

I knew I had a screw knocked loose when the gargoyle stumbled backwards away from her. It made a noise like it was swallowing its own tongue, and Alley Cat shrieked defiantly again.

The gargoyle sprinted to the window, shaking the floor like an elephant come to visit. It crashed through the glass and flew off.

That's when I faded to black.

"It must have been one hell of a party, Bud. Why wasn't I invited?"

I heard the voice, but everything was dark and my head hurt. The kind of hurt you only feel after a three-day bender. The kind of dark you expect when you're dead. I didn't think I was dead, but I vaguely recalled what had transpired before I passed out, so I suspected I might be. I felt like a length of chewed leather.

I opened one eye. It was very bright out there, so I closed it again. A few painful seconds later I chanced both eyes. I saw Kink hovering over me.

"You know, Bud, you spend too much time alone. I worry about the company you keep."

I sat up and regretted it immediately. I don't think there were any parts that *didn't* hurt.

"You're one sorry-looking son of a bitch. I hope she was worth it."

"It wasn't a she this time, Kink. At least I don't think it was."

"Good. I'd hate to think you've slipped so far a dolly could make your face look like leftover lasagna."

I took a look around. Sure enough, by the morning light I could see the place had been ransacked.

"Who's your friend there?"

I looked where she gestured and saw Alley Cat curled up next to me. She was watching Kink with more than casual interest.

"That's Alley Cat," I said, propping myself up against the sofa and lamenting the effort. "I don't know if it was a dream or my imagination or the blows to the head, but I could have sworn I saw her chase off the gargoyle that used me for a speed bag."

"A gargoyle, huh? No wonder you look like shit," said Kink. "But I don't think it was your imagination. Gargoyles are deathly afraid of cats. I'm not too fond of them myself. They tend to confuse me with dinner."

"I'd stay out of range then," I told her. "After watching her stand up to that rock head, I say Alley Cat is pretty tough . . . and probably hungry."

"So what did this gargoyle have against you?"

"It wanted Danny's notebook."

"Why would it want that, and what made it think you had it?"

"I did have it, but I gave it to Danny's editor at the *Specter*."

"How'd you get your paws on it?" wondered Kink.

"Star gave it to me."

"Star? That slinky torch singer down at the *Sanctuary*?"

I nodded.

"How the hell did she get it?"

"It's a long story, Kink, and my head hurts too much. I've got to . . . ."

I tried to get up, but my legs wobbled liked I was a pie-eyed penguin.

"I don't think you've got to do anything but lie down for a while," said Kink. "You might even need a good doc. I'm betting something's broken . . . and not just your pride."

I didn't want to admit it, but she was right. I wasn't going anywhere for a while."

16

DON'T BITE THE MESSENGER

I took off the rest of that day and all of the next to heal up and do some serious drinking. When I say that, I mean I take my drinking seriously. When I get really serious, I've been known to wake up in an Encino fleabag with no shoes and a new tattoo. Fortunately, this time, I was in no shape to go anywhere.

Kink nursed me for a couple of hours, but that was about all she could take. Star called when she got back from Tinseltown. I told her I wasn't feeling well. She wanted to come over, but I insisted I didn't want her to catch whatever I had. The truth is, I didn't want her to see my battered face—not that my everyday mug was going to win any beauty contests. Still, there was nothing she could do, and no reason for me to put that on her.

I wouldn't admit it to myself, but I cared about her. It had been a long time since I'd cared about anything, so I didn't really remember what it felt like. All I knew was that I felt something. What that was . . . well, I didn't put any stock in trying to define it or dissect it.

Early in the third morning after my encounter with old Fists-of-Concrete, I got a call. It was Bruce Barton.

"Dirk, I found your boy—John Prince."

I was up out of my chair, ready to go, before he finished the name. "Where is he?"

"Probably on his way to the morgue by now. He's dead."

"How do you know it's him?"

"I can't be a hundred percent positive. It's just what I'm told by someone I trust. He talked with some other kids who were with him. Apparently the Prince kid OD'd on heeb."

"Alright, Bruce. Thanks. I'll check it out."

I called Doc Pretorius at the coroner's office and told him I might be able to identify a kid they'd found. I asked him not to do anything until I got there. He said it was no problem. Apparently there'd been a run on fresh stiffs lately, and their work was piling up.

The Packard was cold and pouty, probably peeved I hadn't shifted its gears in a while. It wouldn't start at first. I reasoned with it, ranted a bit, and finally it turned over. It was probably just trying to tell me it needed a new battery, so I didn't take it personally.

I got down to the coroner's office as quickly as I could, though I was still moving like a corpse myself. The old doc wasn't a crack coroner for nothing. He noticed right off.

"What meat grinder did you piss off?" he asked when he saw me.

"You should you see the other guy," I countered. "There's not a mark on him."

Doc laughed, thinking I was joking.

"Where's the kid you brought in today?"

He took me into the cold chamber where the bodies were stored. The kid had been stripped and laid out on a table like a side of beef. Except for the track marks on his arms, there wasn't a scratch on him. He looked like he could have been sleeping.

"You know him?" asked Pretorius.

"Yeah." I'd recognized him from his photo right away. "His name is John Prince."

"Not *the* Prince?"

"Yeah. His father hired me to find him."

"Well, you found him."

"What's the cause of death?"

"I'll have to run some tests, but based on those track marks it looks like an OD to me."

"Do me a favor, Doc. Don't call his father yet. I should probably be the one to tell him."

He looked at me like maybe I'd taken one too many blows to the head . . . which I had.

"Alright," he said, shaking his head. "If that's the way you want it. Good luck with that."

"Thanks, Doc."

"He'll still have to come down and make a formal identification."

"I'll tell him."

I wasn't looking forward to telling Dracula that his son was dead, but I figured it was the right thing to do. The truth is, I felt a little guilty. I'd been so distracted looking for Danny's killer, I hadn't spent as much time looking for the kid as I probably should have. I wasn't sure what else I could have done, but I was positive there must have been something. Now he was dead, and there was nothing anyone could do.

On my way to the Prince estate, the rain started up again. I tried not to take it as an omen, even when a murder of crows decided to swoop overhead and drop a few chalky mementos all over my hood.

I'd always wondered about that phrase, "a murder of crows," so I looked it up once. Apparently it originated about four centuries ago, when people began to notice that, after a big bloody battle, flocks of crows would swoop in to feed off the dead. I didn't think it was a fair use of the word. The crows were getting a bum rap. After all, they didn't kill all those people. They were just the cleanup crew.

The guards and their dogs were still patrolling the periphery of Prince's property, the Rolls was still parked out front, and the walk up the stairs to the manor house was still a long one for my bum leg. I was about to ring the bell when a crack of thunder ripped through the gunmetal-gray sky like the devil's whip. It might have been a sign to turn around and go back where I came from, but I decided to ignore it. I pushed the button.

The monastery bells echoed inside the manor as before, but this time Renfield was slow in answering. He opened the double doors and looked at me with some surprise.

"Mr. Slade, the master is not expecting you, is he?"

"No, but I have some . . . news of his son."

"Come in then."

I stepped inside and he closed up behind me.

"I assume you'll be retaining your hat and coat once more."

"Yeah, I'll keep them," I replied, taking off my hat and shaking the rain from it.

He flashed a look of disapproval at the wet floor, but said without any emotion I could detect, "Follow me, please."

He led me to the library again, and in the light of the room he got a better look at me and my battered face. He gestured at the bruises.

"Trouble with the little woman?" he said in as formal a sarcastic tone as I'd ever heard.

"Nope. It was with *his* big brother," I said, pointing at one of the gargoyles on the mantel.

He didn't react. I don't think he believed me. No reason he should. I only half believed me.

"I'll inform the master you are here."

As I waited I was drawn once more to the portrait of Prince that presided over the room. It was a fascinating likeness. So much so, I was certain those coal-black eyes were staring at me, accusing me, condemning me. I half expected the image to come alive and step down from the mantel. I shook my head and countered my paranoia with the awareness that it was simply tinted and dried matter decoratively arranged on a canvas sheet to create a representative manifestation. Any suggestion that it was a living, breathing organism was simply a pigment of my imagination.

Yes, that's the kind of droll P.I. I was. Sometimes even my thoughts arranged themselves as puns.

"Renfield says you have news of John."

He swept into the room, not in a smoking jacket this time, but a dark business suit. He stood there, staring at me, not unlike his portrait. I guess I was caught off guard, because I didn't answer right away.

"Mr. Slade, I'm already late for an important meeting," he said in that quiet but commanding voice of his. "What have you learned about my son?"

I would have preferred he was sitting down, but I could see that wasn't happening. I cleared my throat.

"I'm afraid I have bad news, Mr. Prince. Your son is dead."

He didn't collapse or stagger. He barely moved at all. The only sign he understood what I'd said was a slight downward cast of his eyes.

"Are you certain?"

"Yes, I'm sure of it. I saw him myself."

He drifted over to the lone window in the room as if being carried by the wind. He stared out at the rain.

"In one sense I'm not surprised. I only asked because I wasn't certain . . ." He paused as if it were difficult to get the words out. "I didn't know for a fact that John *could* die, being my son."

I knew the old stories about Prince's longevity, his rumored immortality—not that I believed them. Still, it still seemed a strange thing for him to say.

"All I know is the coroner has pronounced him dead," I said. "You'll have to go in to make an official identification and see to arrangements."

"Yes, of course."

"I'm sorry . . . ." I stopped, then started again. "I'm sorry I didn't find him before . . . before this happened."

"I'm sure you did everything you could," he said, still gazing outside.

I knew I hadn't done enough, but I figured falling on my sword at that moment wouldn't do anyone any good.

"All I wanted was his respect," he muttered as if no one else were in the room. He turned back to me. "How did he die?"

"It was an overdose. From the looks of it, he'd been using for some time."

"Drugs?"

He seemed surprised by this. Most parents are.

"I'm afraid so. It was a new drug that's circulating the streets. It's called heeb. I'm not sure what it is exactly, but I know it's been making the rounds, pushed by local gangs."

He looked at me with more interest and emotion than he'd shown so far.

"What gangs?"

"I learned John had been hanging out with a group known as the Fiends. They were selling the stuff, distributing it for Boss Wolf—a local hood named Larry Talbot."

"Talbot?" The refined, tranquil expression that never seemed to leave his face retreated like the wicked witch from a shower. I couldn't tell if the new countenance he wore was colored with anger or guilt . . . or both.

"Yeah. He's not the kind of guy who hangs out in your social circles, so you've probably never heard of him." Even as I said it, I could see Prince *had* heard of him. He knew the name and, apparently knew it more than casually.

His businesslike manner and unruffled demeanor returned as quickly as it had fled.

"Thank you for coming out to tell me yourself, Mr. Slade. I appreciate it. You may give Renfield an invoice for your services. I'm afraid I have to fly. I'm already very late."

Before I could hem and haw about not taking his money for such an outcome, he was gone. It was a good thing, because I could really use the dough, no matter how guilty I felt.

Still, I found his turn from cold to hot to cold again peculiar, even for an odd old duck like him. I couldn't help but wonder when and where he'd crossed paths with Talbot. Wolfman meets Dracula? It must have been a sequel I wasn't familiar with.

111

17

HOWLING AT THE MOON

On my way back from giving Prince the bad news, I started thinking about Star. It was funny how I couldn't get her out of my head. I thought I was past the age where a dame could affect me like that. Apparently I wasn't. Somewhere along the road, I decided she was basically a good kid. She'd had her trials and tribulations in life, but who hadn't? Shortly after the rain stopped, I came to the conclusion she didn't deserve to have those films held over her head for the rest of her life. She certainly didn't deserve to be Talbot's puppet.

It might have been my own tarnished armor I was trying to polish, but I decided to do something about it. I made up my mind to go see Talbot and get those reels back. Of course, I had no idea *how* I was going to do it. I knew he wouldn't just give them to me out of the kindness of his gypsy-cursed heart. He'd want something in return. That made it easy, because I didn't have anything. All I had was me. Maybe I could offer him my services—just say I'll owe him. He might go for that . . . and he might laugh me out his house.

It didn't matter. That's where I was headed. And once I made up my mind, I was like a freight train. I had a full head of steam and a pigheaded optimism that the tracks were clear. It made no difference to me if the bridge up ahead was as rickety as an octogenarian's legs.

So I was on my way to confront Boss Wolf when I saw smoke rising in the pallid moonlight. It was billowing up from somewhere in my own neighborhood, so I detoured to see what was burning. It wasn't long before I saw the fire truck lights and the rabble that had gathered to gawk.

I hit the brakes when I saw what was still burning. It was *Maddie's Place*.

The fire crew, led by Chief Van Helsing, was still valiantly fighting the blaze, but I could see it was a lost cause.

Desperately I searched the faces of the onlookers. Thankfully I spotted Maddie sitting on the curb. Her face and clothes were covered in soot, and an ambulance medic was treating her right arm for burns. I went to her.

"Are you okay, Maddie?" It was a stupid question, but the first thing out of my mouth.

She was just sitting there, staring at the fire, paying no attention to the medic. She didn't acknowledge me either. I could see she was in shock.

The medic finished wrapping her arm and went back to his ambulance for something. I sat down next to her and took her hand. She still had no idea I was there. Apparently entranced by the flames, she spoke barely loud enough to be heard over the tumult.

"They burned it down," she said, more to herself than me. "Burned it down because I wouldn't sell. Burned it all."

Before I could ask who "they" were, Frank Stein came running up and shoved me out of the way. He fell to his knees and took Maddie in his arms as delicately as the big lug could. He stroked her hair and whispered soothingly in her ear. I couldn't hear what he said, but I knew he still carried a sizable torch for her—even though they hadn't been together in a long time.

There was nothing for me to do. I left them alone and got back in the Packard.

I knew what Maddie was talking about. Whether she was right or just traumatized, I wouldn't even try to guess. Would someone really burn down her place because she wouldn't sell? Then what would they have—an empty lot? Even if they could buy it then, what good was it?

By the time I got to Talbot's house, the visibility was making it hard to drive. The cloud cover had descended, morphing into a thick fog, consuming much of the city. Talbot lived on a hill, and the closer I got to his place, the harder it was to see. The only thing I could make out was the full moon, peeking in and out of the gloom as if afraid to show its face.

As I approached the house, it occurred to me that a full-moon night might not be the best time to engage Boss Wolf. It wasn't much more than a passing thought, but it was there.

The truth is, after all my time in Monster Town, I still didn't know what was real and what was only cinematic special effects. I'd certainly seen some bizarre things, so nothing was out of the question.

I pulled up and parked. I was here, so I was going in—moonlight and curses be damned. It did briefly occur to me that a few silver bullets right about then would have been nice . . . even if I had to throw them.

The first sign of trouble I spotted was nothing. That is, there were no guards on the place. I would have expected one or two outside at least. I was right about that. When I got closer I observed a pair of legs sticking out from the shrubbery. They weren't moving.

I downshifted and moved in more cautiously. From inside the house I heard a resounding growl, followed by a raucous crash. There was an ongoing fight. It was such a wild clamor, my still-aching bones were glad they were where they were. Still, I had to know what was going on. I stole closer to a window, but could see very little through the curtains there. I heard a sharp yelp, then nothing—just silence. The fight was over.

I continued around the house. There was a car in the driveway outside the double garage. I couldn't quite make it out in the murk until its engine started and its lights came on. I wasn't able to see who was behind the wheel, but I recognized the flying rodent hood ornament. It was Prince's Rolls Royce.

It sped off and I hurried inside the door that had been left wide open.

There'd been a hellacious fight inside for sure. The furniture was in splinters, the walls had holes bashed into them, and there were bloodstains on the carpet.

I followed the trail of havoc right to Talbot's body. Only he wasn't Talbot, he was the Wolfman—fully transformed. His throat had been ripped to shreds.

He'd gotten in his licks. There were bits of flesh on his spiked fingernails and in his teeth, but strangely no residue of blood.

There was no doubt that whoever, or whatever, had taken him down had been wounded as well. Even so, I wondered who could have possibly been powerful enough to take out Boss Wolf like that. Yeah, I saw the car, and I knew Prince's legendary reputation, but anyone could have been driving that Rolls. It was difficult to imagine the slender, somewhat effeminate Prince doing that to Talbot.

I didn't have much time to ponder it. Something jumped me— literally jumped on my back, snarling like a wild animal. It was Leech Woman. She was naked as far as I could see, her legs wrapped around my middle, one arm locked across my chest, a brass letter opener in her free hand. Taking a page out of her own script, she was trying to stab me in the back of the neck.

Her first slash caught my falling fedora. It probably saved my life. By the time she'd disengaged her blade from my hat, I'd pulled her legs loose and tossed her over my head. She fell flat, dropping her weapon in the process. It took her a couple of seconds to recover, but she wasn't done with me. She got to her feet and shot me a look of hatred.

It was obvious she thought I'd killed Talbot. She'd probably gone into hiding when she first heard the fight, and only emerged when it got quiet.

I would have pointed out to her that there was no way I could have done that to Talbot, and that I didn't have a drop of blood on me, but she never gave me the chance.

She charged me like a rabid dog, and I only had a moment to admire her buxom figure before I decked her. She went down and out.

115

I picked up my fedora. It was done for. I took it with me anyway, so if she went to the police, it would be her word against mine that I was ever there. I didn't think she would.

Then I got out of there, pronto.

I knew I'd never catch the Rolls, but where it was going was no secret. The question of who was driving it, who knocked off Boss Wolf, wasn't as important as why. If it wasn't Prince, it was probably someone or some *thing* doing his bidding. Was it a matter of business gone bad? Were Prince and Talbot involved in something shady? Or did Prince simply blame Talbot for the death of his son?

I knew I wasn't going to figure it all out that night, so I headed for Star's place. Only when I arrived, she wasn't there . . . or she wasn't answering her door. Of course that last supposition was just my paranoia rearing its repugnant head again. I had trust issues, and at the moment, my brain still occupied with trying to unravel the twisted threads of this convoluted case, I would have suspected Kink of being a closeted nun.

I finally said, "The hell with it all," and went home.

18

STAR-CROSSED

Until I saw the Rolls outside Talbot's place, I had no reason to suspect Prince of anything. He was just a guy who hired me to find his missing son. A very rich guy. I still wasn't certain he *was* involved in anything, except for Talbot's murder. And that could have been strictly payback for his son's death. I had no evidence of any other connection, but my P.I. nose was smelling something. I just didn't know if it was *Eau d'Vengeance* or *L'Air du Conspiracy*.

That all changed when I got a call from Igor at *The Daily Specter*. I'd asked him to find out what he could about Black Castle Attractions, the corporation that was buying up Monster Town. What he told me was that it was a newly formed company, incorporated only in the last year, and based in Los Angeles. He confirmed he'd found verification they'd been buying land in Monster Town, and gave me a list of the company's officers—which were also its main shareholders. It was a short list, and I wasn't as surprised as I might have been a week ago, to learn that Vladimir Prince was on it.

It was no secret Prince ran several companies, and for many years had owned various properties in Monster Town. But his connection with Black Castle and its acquisitions had all occurred recently.

So, at the same time this company was buying up Monster Town, blatant crime was on the rise and someone wanted the public to know about the toxic water. You didn't have to be a mad scientist to connect the body parts.

It almost surely meant Prince had made some kind of deal with Talbot, who in turn hired Hyde and his Fiends to stir up trouble. Enough trouble to frighten the general public—monster or not.

The pieces seemed to fit, but what I didn't understand was *why*. It made sense to lower property values and give people an incentive to leave town in order to buy their property, but then you'd own a lot of worthless land. Obviously Prince and his partners had plenty of dough, and were certain they were going to make a boatload more, or they wouldn't be involved. I just had no clue what their end game could possibly be.

The only thing I was sure of was that I needed to get inside Prince's home to take a good look around. That would be no simple task. With the security he had outside, getting in wouldn't be easy. Even the Invisible Man couldn't get by the dogs. The only way to avoid them would be to come in by air. Unfortunately, I was short one silent helicopter.

I couldn't think of a way to avoid getting my ass chewed off, so I let the idea ride. I decided to call Star. I figured a little company might do me some good, but she still wasn't answering. So I headed over to the *Sanctuary*, hoping she might be there. She wasn't.

I parked myself at the bar and ordered a drink. Quasi told me he hadn't seen Star in a couple of days, but that it wasn't unusual. Her deal with the band was an on and off kind of thing. She'd been upfront about having to go away once and while for auditions. I didn't have *any* deal with her, so I had no gripe that she seemed to have disappeared.

I nursed my Scotch and thought about the problem of getting into Prince's place. Kink certainly couldn't carry me. I'd need someone with wings who was a lot bigger and stronger.

"Hey, Quasi, know any trustworthy gargoyles who might want to earn a little extra dough?"

"A gargoyle?" He looked at me like I'd had one too many, even though he knew it was my first. "Are you kidding? What do you need a gargoyle for?"

"I want to drop in unexpectedly on a friend," I said. "You know, from on high."

"I get it, but *trustworthy* and *gargoyle* aren't really two words that go together. One would just as likely take your money, then drop you on your head. Where is it you're trying to sneak into, Slade?"

"I need to get inside Vladimir Prince's mansion to have a look around."

"That doesn't sound like a real bright thing to do," he replied.

"No, it's not," I agreed.

"But if you're bent on being stupid, I might have a way for you to get in."

"Yeah? How's that?"

"Prince is throwing this big shindig at his place tomorrow night, and one of our new owners arranged for Sonny D and the Night Dogs to play at the party. I guess he's a friend of Prince's, or a business associate or something."

"Okay, but how does that get me in?"

"I don't know." He shrugged. "You play any kind of musical instrument?"

When I was a kid, my mother made me take clarinet lessons. I was so bad she didn't try to stop me when I quit. I doubted time had made me any better . . . even if I remembered where my fingers went— which I didn't.

Quasi went off to wait on some other customers. I considered his idea. I didn't necessarily have to perform with the band. I just had to get inside. Afterwards no one would be likely to notice one less band member.

I'd have to talk to Gil, a.k.a. Sonny D, about it, but I figured he'd be okay with it, as long as I didn't tell him why I was crashing the party. Besides, he owed me. I'd have to have a disguise though. I wasn't quite sure how you disguised a six-foot-three, 220-pound, broken-nosed, crew cut P.I. with a limp. Maybe Kink had a special kind of fairy dust that would do the job.

Gil Mckenna was basically a good guy. His one run at the movies, *The Hideous Sun Demon*, was a nuclear bomb. He'd managed to stay in show business using his musical talents, and as long as he stayed out of the sun, he wasn't homicidal or hideous. In fact, he was fairly good looking.

He agreed to sneak me into Prince's party with the band, if I promised not to finger him if I got caught. He also solved the problem of my disguise. The band still had one of their previous piano player's outfits. With the Phantom of the Opera's mask and cape I could walk right in. It was a formal party, so everyone would be in tuxes—even the band. Once I managed to slip away and get rid of the mask and cape, I'd look just like any other party guest. Unless I ran into Renfield or Prince or his steamy young squeeze, Mina. That was okay. I didn't plan on spending much time at the party itself. I wanted to have a closer look at whatever was in Prince's desk in the library. I realized what I was looking for might not be there, but it was as good a place as any to start.

The band used an old bakery van to haul their instruments, and I crowded it a bit, even though the new piano man wasn't with us. Gil and the Mad Ghoul were up front, and Mickey the Troll climbed into the back because he wanted to hold on to his precious bass. I squeezed into the backseat between the Mummy and the ice creature, whose name I didn't catch. I didn't mind, even though I was getting freezer burn on one side and a sprinkling of dry rot and dust on the other.

The band got there early to set up and do their sound check, but they weren't the only early arrivals. A couple limos were already out front when we pulled up. As I was helping the Mummy carry in his drum set, I came up behind another tuxedoed guest. He gave his name to Renfield at the door and was escorted to the library.
I recognized the name. It was one of those on the list of corporate officers Igor had relayed to me.

I put down the drum like I needed a rest and watched Renfield open the library door for the newcomer. I only got a glimpse, but I saw a few other guests already inside. I figured Prince was in there too. It was where I needed to be, but there was no way I was getting in, or even getting close enough to hear what they were saying. I'd have to bide my time.

I didn't have to wait long. The place filled up in a hurry. I'd never seen so many penguins roosting in one place. That was a good thing for me. I'd be able to blend in like a tree in the forest.

Even without the monkey suits and limos you would have known the guests were made of money. There was an air about them, a certain confidence. Maybe it was arrogance. Maybe it was obvious they were rich old men because most of them had younger wives. Normally I would have enjoyed the scenery, but I had work to do.

I slipped into the bathroom designated for the help as soon as the band started to play. I ditched the cape and mask in the back of a closet and came out as myself. The first thing I did was locate Renfield. He was stationed near the main entrance to the ballroom. Fortunately, it wasn't the only entrance—or exit. When I saw Prince lead his business partners into the party, I knew his little meeting was over. I watched and waited for an opportunity. I kept on the move, doing my best to keep away from Prince and his butler. When I saw my chance, I made a casual dash for the library. There was no one inside. I shut the door behind me.

I was almost disappointed with what I found. There were no arcane riddles to be deciphered, no books that had to be tilted to reveal a hidden room, no secret passageways to discover. I didn't even have to jimmy open a locked drawer. Spread across Prince's desk was a large blueprint of just what I was looking for. I knew it was, because I recognized the names of certain Monster Town streets. The plots were differentiated by markings. From what I already knew, it looked like the difference was between what parcels of land they already owned and what they didn't. What I couldn't figure out, was what exactly they were planning to build. Whatever it was, it was huge. No wonder they needed so much property.

I was trying so hard to figure it out, I guess I didn't hear the door open.

"I was looking for Vlad, but you'll do."

It was Prince's pale young mistress. She was decked out in a snow-white evening gown and pearls. She sashayed towards me, smiling like a sphinx that had swallowed a flock of canaries.

"Are you my birthday present?" she said, sizing me up.

If it was her birthday, I figured she must be the reason for the party. I played along.

"I don't think so, but we might be able to work something out later."

"I think I'd like to unwrap you now," she purred. "I'll go ask Vlad if it's okay." She turned toward the open door.

I didn't think she was really going. It was a bluff, but I couldn't chance it. I hurried over as fast as my bum leg would take me, saying, "Wait." I took her arm and turned her to face me. Off the top of my head, I couldn't think of much to stall her. So I said, "I guess a birthday kiss wouldn't be out of the question."

She smiled and leaned in on her tiptoes. I obliged. I'd meant to give her a brotherly peck, but we ended up in a full clinch. When I came up for air, I barely had time to notice the look of surprise on her face before I noticed the aroma of gun oil. The realization coincided with the lights going out.

It was still dark when I began to shake the cobwebs from my skull. My head pounded like an angry judge's gavel. I couldn't move my arms or my legs, and my butt itched like the devil. More than anything, I was steamed. I was tired of people beating on me like they were tenderizing a steak.

When the pounding faded to a light throb I strained to listen. I could hear music far away. The party was still going on somewhere above me. I hadn't been out that long.

Gradually my eyes adjusted and I could see I was tied to a sturdy chair in Prince's wine cellar. The heavy chair wouldn't rock and I couldn't move much more than my aching head. Someone had cold-cocked me good. I guessed from the scent I'd caught before I went down that it was Renfield.

He hogtied me rather efficiently too. I wasn't going anywhere, so I listened again, more carefully this time, to see if I was alone. I heard a scurrying noise and something else I couldn't identify. Whether it was rats or bats didn't matter much.

I sat there quite a while, tied up like Houdini, but without any of his escape artist expertise. That didn't stop me from twisting and pulling at the ropes. I was the proverbial fly, just waiting for the spider to make its entrance. The thing was, I hated waiting. I always had. Sedentary thumb-twiddling wasn't my cup of joe. I guess I found sitting around doing nothing too akin to death. Subconsciously, I guess I figured if you kept moving, the Reaper could never get a clear shot at you. Though, at that moment, the symbolism seemed a little too apropos.

Not that I had much choice. All I could do was cool my heels until the heat came down. So I waited . . . and waited. The minutes crawled by like a wounded cockroach.

Finally I heard a door open. The music was a little louder for a moment. A dim light came on. Renfield walked in, an old German Luger in his hand. He pointed it at me like I might suddenly fly away. Prince followed him in.

"Mr. Slade, I thought we'd concluded our business," said Prince nonchalantly.

"I just thought I'd drop by, pick up my check, and wish Miss Mina a happy birthday."

"Yes, Renfield told me about your birthday greeting for her. Naughty, naughty, Mr. Slade."

"She practically begged for it. It would have been impolite to refuse."

"Politeness didn't seem to concern you when you intruded upon my party without an invitation."

"I figured it just got lost in the mail."

He walked partway around me like he was stalking prey.

"You consider yourself quite a wit, don't you, Mr. Slade?"

I was trying to prove his point by thinking up something particularly clever to say when I heard the door open again. I looked over as best I could in my restrained condition, but didn't see anyone come out of the dark.

"Come in, my dear, come in," said Prince. "I believe you know our uninvited visitor."

She walked in, dressed to the nines like all of his the guests. It was Star.

"Did you search him?" Prince asked Renfield as if it had just occurred to him.

"He doesn't carry a gun," said Star. Renfield nodded.

I was still wrapping my head around her presence, when Prince asked me, "So what is it that you were looking for tonight, Mr. Slade? What is it, exactly, that you think you know?"

"I know you're buying up as much real estate in Monster Town as you can. Despite what I was told," I said, staring daggers at Star, "I'm guessing you were the one who passed the information about the poisonous water to my friend Danny that got him killed."

"I was just doing my civic duty. We regularly test the water at my brewery, or I would never have known about it. I am sorry about your friend though. I was only hoping he'd publish the story. I had no idea another faction would try to silence him."

I expected smug satisfaction, but instead Star looked contrite. I wasn't buying it. It wasn't the first time I'd been stung by a perfect ass, but it was the first time I'd felt like one.

"I'm also pretty sure," I continued, "that you're behind the recent crime spree in Monster Town. Between the bad water and the crime, you figured you'd pick up your property at bargain basement prices."

"Very good, Mr. Slade. I can see why you're such a competent investigator. You've got it all figured out."

"Except for one thing," I said, still trying to wriggle my hands free with no luck. "I don't know what it is you expect to do with all that underpriced land. What's the grift?"

"You don't?" He was beaming now. "Why that's the best part, Mr. Slade. We're going to build an enormous amusement park. People will come from all over the country—all over the world—to visit. They'll bring their children, their grandmothers, their brothers and sisters. They'll spend millions. Someday maybe billions."

His close-set black eyes had dollar signs in them. I didn't know why. Amusement parks were a dime a dozen. They couldn't make that much. I didn't get the angle. Then he told me.

"Do you know what we're going to call it, Mr. Slade?"

"Hopscotch World?"

"No, Mr. Slade. It's going to be called *Monster Land*."

He let that sink in a moment, and it did. I could see the appeal right away.

"Just imagine it. There will be rides based on all the greatest monster movies, with many of the actual monsters in attendance. If we can't get the real thing, we'll hire actors. It won't just be rides though. We'll have sets designed with the latest technology to look exactly like scenes from the most frightening horror films of all time. Visitors will be able to walk into and explore Baron von Frankenstein's castle, the Abominable Snowman's icy lair, the Mummy's ancient tomb, the Creature's underwater caverns. They'll think it's fun—just looking around. Then they'll get the scare of their lives. People love to be scared, Mr. Slade. The movies prove it. They'll come again and again. The merchandising alone will pay off the initial investment."

The music upstairs had ceased while he was talking. Renfield noticed and whispered something in Prince's ear when he finally took a breath from his zealous sales pitch.

"Yes, yes," he said to his servant. Then to me, "I'm afraid I need to speak to a few of my guests before they leave, Mr. Slade. You won't go anywhere, will you? I'd like to finish our chat."

I tried to shrug but couldn't.

"Renfield, give your weapon to Miss Starlin. He looks fairly well incapacitated, but we don't want to take any chances."

125

Renfield did not look at all happy about giving up his gun, but he obeyed.

"If he should somehow get loose, my dear, please shoot him."

She took the gun, but held it like it might bite her. It wasn't until she actually had it in her hand that I was sure about her. I guess I still didn't want to believe she'd duped me.

"You work for him," I said, stating the obvious.

"Of course she does. Most everyone in Monster Town works for me, one way or another, including you, Mr. Slade."

"Not anymore," I said with more defiance than I felt.

"We'll discuss that when I get back." He turned and left with Renfield following.

I looked at Star. Her eyes were wet with unshed tears. Something about her got to me. I couldn't believe I still felt sorry for her. I tried to shake it off.

"You played me," I said. "You played me good."

"No I didn't!" she yelled back at me.

"You were never working for Boss Wolf. All this time you've been working for the real master."

"That's not true. I *was* working for Talbot. Vlad sent me to him to keep an eye on what he was doing."

"So it's *Vlad*, is it? How chummy are you two?"

"It's not like that," she insisted quietly.

"What about the films you told me Talbot had? The ones he was supposedly blackmailing you with."

"He did have them, but Vlad got them from him and burned them."

"So what? You owed him?"

"Yes, I owed him," she said defiantly. "But that wasn't the only reason I did what he wanted me to. He gave me a look at myself I've never had before. He saw something in me nobody else ever did. He made me see it too. He made me believe it."

At that point I wasn't even sure if she realized she was reciting lines from *A Star is Born*, but I called her on it anyway.

"Nice try, but I've seen that movie too."

She made a noise like she was exasperated—frustrated that I didn't understand.

"He's going to use some of the profits from *Monster Land* to produce a movie just for me. A real film, not a nudie pic or a B-movie, but a legitimate film. I'll finally get my chance to be a real actress, like Susan Hayward in *I'll Cry Tomorrow* or Judy Holliday in *Born Yesterday*."

I could see she was still blinded by the stardust in her eyes. She couldn't see that even Prince, with all his dough, couldn't give her what she wanted.

"Star, don't you . . . ." I didn't finish because I didn't really know what to say. There was nothing *to* say.

"What's cooking, Bud?"

Kink suddenly appeared out of nowhere.

"What are you doing here, Kink? Did you just decide to tune in to my frequency?"

"Nah. Quasi told me what kind of craziness you were up to. Since I'm the craziest girl you know, I thought I'd pop in and see if I could help. Looks like you need it." It was only then she noticed Star standing there. "What's *she* doing here?" asked Kink with the usual possessive distrust she had concerning me and other women. "What's she doing with that gun?"

At that moment I heard Prince and Renfield returning.

"Hide, Kink," I whispered as loud as I dared. "Hide now."

Kink buzzed off into a dark corner. I couldn't see where. Prince walked straight up to me. I didn't think he'd seen Kink.

"Mr. Slade, I've decided it's probably for the best if we terminate our relationship. *Monster Land* is a foregone conclusion at this point. We've already secured most of the properties we need, and it's unlikely you could do anything to impede us. But I had to ask myself, why take that chance? There's just too much at stake. So I'm going have Renfield see to you." He gestured to Star. "Give Renfield the gun, my dear, and come along. There are still some people upstairs I'd like to introduce you to. Some people who could be very good for your career."

Renfield walked over to get his Luger, but Star took a step back.

"You don't have to do this, Vlad. This private dick is nothing. He can't stop you. Just let him go."

"What's this? It almost sounds as if you care, my dear. Come now, no more nonsense. Give it to Renfield and let's go upstairs."

Renfield tried to take the gun, but Star wouldn't hand it over. He grabbed at her, and then Kink suddenly swooped down like a hawk on a rabbit. She buzzed Renfield's tower and let go a trail of fairy dust across his eyes. He tried to bat her away, but she was already gone. Half blind, he reached for the gun again. It went off. Renfield went down.

Star stood there, seemingly in shock, the Luger still smoking in her hand. Her face was as white as a ghost.

"You shouldn't have done that, Janice." Prince's tone had changed. The smarminess was gone, replaced by something more than just vaguely sinister. "Renfield has been with me a very long time. He won't easily be replaced. Now give me the gun." He took two very smooth steps towards her. "Give me the gun," he repeated.

Star didn't move. Her eyes didn't even focus. I couldn't tell if she was still in shock or if Prince had somehow mesmerized her. He moved closer.

"Star!" I bellowed. "Star, wake up!"

"Give me the gun," he said again. "You can't hurt me with it. Give it to me."

Kink came out of nowhere again, dive-bombing Prince like a crazed Stuka. He lost his focus and swatted at Kink. He missed, but she came back again, and this time he connected with the back of his hand. Kink hurdled across the room. I couldn't see where she landed.

It had been enough. Star was back. She had the Luger pointed at Prince.

"Bullets won't hurt me, my dear." He took another step closer. "Give me the gun and we'll forget this ever happened."

She fired twice, then once more—I guess because he didn't go right down.

Prince stood there as if all the legends about him were true. The sound of gunshots had given me brief hope, but when he didn't fall, I figured we were lost.

"You can't . . . kill me," said Prince, looking down at the holes in his chest. "I can't . . . ." Before he could elaborate on his invulnerability, he fell to the floor. It was more of a thud than a splat, but he was down and he wasn't moving.

"Untie me, quick!" I said to Star.

This time she didn't hesitate. She rushed to my side, dropped the gat, and started working on the knots. While she did, I had time to worry about Kink.

"Kink? Kink, where are you?"

"Right here, Bud."

She flew into my view, a little wobbly but in one piece.

"Check him, Kink. Is he dead?"

She fluttered over and took a look at Prince.

"He looks dead, but I don't see any blood."

Dead or not, I didn't want to hang around and try to explain everything to the cops. Finally free, I tried rubbing the circulation back into my arms and said, "Let's blow this joint."

19

THAT'S ANOTHER STORY

I woke up the next morning in my own bed, with my arm around Star, her lovely posterior pressed up against me. I felt a call to action but decided to let her sleep. I rolled over and thought about where the last couple of weeks had taken me.

My best friend, Danny, was dead. For that matter, so was the Invisible Man, Dr. Jekyll, the Wolfman, Renfield, the son of Dracula, and, as far as I knew, Dracula himself. It was a lot of bodies for a fortnight. What bothered me most was that one of Danny's killers was still out here. I wouldn't let him go. I'd track him down eventually—as soon as I figured out how to bring down a 400-pound gargoyle.

As for Star, I didn't know if she and I were going anywhere special, but I reckoned I was along for the ride . . . at least until I got thrown. I calculated we had only a 50-50 chance at something that would last. Still, when you let the numbers start to run you, it was time to take your money off the table. Uncertainty was life's only guarantee.

I got out of bed. I limped a little more than usual over to my clothes and quietly cursed my aging body. My concern about Star was probably wasted worry. Chances were, long before she tired of me, my old heart would give out trying to keep up with her.

I got dressed and went out to find a paper.

It was there, on the front page of *The Daily Specter*, the story about the city's water. It covered it all—the unrevealed tests, Jekyll's silence, the involvement of the governor's office in the cover-up, and even the murder of reporter Danny Legget. I was happy to see that last part. Danny deserved the credit. I thought it was important for people to know that he died doing something he believed in. Igor did a good job with it.

As for the scheme to lower property values and buy up Monster

Town, that was another story. I would tell Igor what I knew about it, but he'd be on his own. I didn't have any proof. All I had was what they call hearsay. Yet with Igor on the case, I didn't think they'd be able to whitewash it.

I wondered, if Prince were truly dead, would the other investors go ahead with their plans for a grand amusement park that would swallow up Monster Town for good? Or would that monument to greed die with him? That morning's article would certainly further their ambitions—at least for the moment. There would be a lot more people willing to pack up and leave now that they knew the water was toxic. I figured I'd stay. Until they cleaned things up, I'd just drink my Scotch straight.

Even so, I gave Monster Town less of a chance than me and Star. But I'd always leaned to the cynical side. I guess that's how life groomed me. I'd seen war, murder, man's continued inhumanity to man, and monstrous mayhem of all kinds. Yet with all I'd seen, all I'd learned over the past couple of weeks, I had new questions about where the world was headed . . . and who the real monsters were.

"Hey, Bud." Kink settled on the edge of my newspaper and tried to read it upside down. "What you reading?"

"Better read it for yourself, Kink. You won't want to be drinking the water anytime soon."

"Never touch the stuff," she boasted. "And don't call me Kink anymore. I'm back to Wink now. I'm going straight. Going to make kiddie movies again."

I couldn't have been more dumbfounded if a parade of undead dressed for St. Patrick's Day came marching down the street.

"You really think they'll let you?"

"Hell no," she said, hovering next to my face. "I was just yanking your chain. They'd never give me any screen time again. But don't you think Wink is the perfect name for a private eye?"

I was still thinking about what had gone down, and I tended to only hear about half of what Kink ever said anyway, because I could still get all I really needed to hear from half. Then my brain caught up with her words and did a double take.

"What did you say?"

"I said I'm going to be your new partner. *Wink and Slade*—sounds pretty good, doesn't it?"

All it took was the slightest thought of going back to work. That forlorn saxophone was back in my head, full of mystery and danger, wailing for all it was worth—the soundtrack of my life.

As for Kink, I knew her notions were as flighty and mutable as the weather. The next week she'd just as likely want to build a rocket ship that could fly her to the moon . . . or something equally crazy. But I figured I'd give her this moment.

"Well, what do you think?" she pressed, buzzing about in front of me—first left, then right, then left again—like a bumblebee on Benzedrine.

"Sure, Wink. That's jake with me."

ACKNOWLEDGEMENTS

First I want to express my gratitude to Pete Crowther, Scott Jones, Nicky Crowther, Mike Smith, Tamsin Traves, and all the folks at PS Publishing for their professionalism and amenability in shepherding the first edition of this book to publication. Along with cover artist Ben Baldwin, they created a beautiful hardback edition of *Monster Town*. Without them, I likely never would have gotten the chance to see my book for sale online sitting right next to one of Stephen King's novels. I also would never have caught the eye of a London TV producer at Roughcut Publications, who optioned the book for a possible TV series.

In addition, I want to thank Darlene Santori, Steve Vaughn, Linda Bona, and Cecilia Vaughn for some of the creative threads that helped sew the pieces of this monster together. And I especially want to thank Carolyn Crow, for not only her creative input, but for finding many of those devilish typos that seem to haunt me more and more as Father Time takes his toll.

Finally, I want to thank Raymond Chandler, Mary Shelley, Dashiell Hammett, Bram Stoker, and Mickey Spillane for helping to create the genres that I attempted to satirize in this book. I would like to think they'd consider it an *hommagé*.

ABOUT THE AUTHOR

The initial publication of *Monster Town* coincided with Bruce Golden's 40th year as a professional writer. He made his first freelance sale to the national political magazine *The Progressive* in late 1976, while still a student at San Diego State University. "Swimsuit Optional Zone" was an article about the nation's only legal nude beach. Since then, his byline has appeared on more than 300 published works of both non-fiction and fiction (the thousands of stories for broadcast he's written are on their way to the constellation Ursa Major by now).

Bruce's short stories have been published more than a 150 times across a score of countries and in more than three dozen anthologies. His work as a satirist has been given life in both print and on air, including his creation of *Radio Free Comedy* in 1994.

You can learn more about Bruce's other books by searching Amazon.com or going to:

http://goldentales.tripod.com/

Made in the USA
Coppell, TX
14 January 2020

14498091R00075